THE RAKE MISTAKE

HEIST CLUB #1

ERICA RIDLEY

Copyright © 2021 Erica Ridley
Design © Erica Ridley

This is a work of fiction. Names, characters, places, and incidents are the product of the author's imagination or are used fictitiously. Any resemblance to actual events, locales, or persons, living or dead, is purely coincidental.

All rights reserved. Except as permitted under the U.S. Copyright Act of 1976, no part of this publication may be reproduced, distributed, or transmitted in any form or by any means, or stored in a database or retrieval system, without the prior written permission of the author.

ALSO BY ERICA RIDLEY

The *Dukes of War*:
The Viscount's Tempting Minx (FREE!)
The Earl's Defiant Wallflower
The Captain's Bluestocking Mistress
The Major's Faux Fiancée
The Brigadier's Runaway Bride
The Pirate's Tempting Stowaway
The Duke's Accidental Wife
A Match, Unmasked
All I Want

The *Wild Wynchesters*:
The Governess Gambit (FREE!)
The Duke Heist
The Perks of Loving a Wallflower
Nobody's Princess

***Heist Club*:**
The Rake Mistake
The Modiste Mishap

***Rogues to Riches*:**

Lord of Chance
Lord of Pleasure
Lord of Night
Lord of Temptation
Lord of Secrets
Lord of Vice
Lord of the Masquerade

The *12 Dukes of Christmas*:
Once Upon a Duke (FREE!)
Kiss of a Duke
Wish Upon a Duke
Never Say Duke
Dukes, Actually
The Duke's Bride
The Duke's Embrace
The Duke's Desire
Dawn With a Duke
One Night With a Duke
Ten Days With a Duke
Forever Your Duke
Making Merry

***Gothic Love Stories*:**
Too Wicked to Kiss
Too Sinful to Deny

Too Tempting to Resist

Too Wanton to Wed

Too Brazen to Bite

Magic & Mayhem:

Kissed by Magic

Must Love Magic

Smitten by Magic

The *Siren's Retreat* Quartet

A Tryst by the Sea by Grace Burrowes

An Affair by the Sea by Erica Ridley

A Spinster by the Sea by Grace Burrowes

Love Letters by the Sea by Erica Ridley

The *Wicked Dukes Club*:

One Night for Seduction by Erica Ridley

One Night of Surrender by Darcy Burke

One Night of Passion by Erica Ridley

One Night of Scandal by Darcy Burke

One Night to Remember by Erica Ridley

One Night of Temptation by Darcy Burke

THE RAKE MISTAKE

CHAPTER 1

June 19, 1817
London, England

iss Philippa York could not wait for her friends to arrive.

Being trapped in her parents' fashionable Mayfair town house day after day was dull enough to make her scream. The one bright exception was her Thursday afternoon reading circle.

"What in heaven's name are you doing?" gasped her mother from the parlor's open doorway. "Arranging furniture is for maids and footmen! It is *conduct unbecoming* a lady."

"The staff prepared the room," Philippa assured her. "I'm... refining the pattern."

Two dozen deep, comfortable armchairs faced

each other in a large oval. It was a perfectly acceptable distribution of chairs.

Philippa had tired of things that were merely acceptable. She'd been accepting them all of her life. She wanted something bigger. Something *different*.

But if all she could have was a Thursday afternoon reading circle, then she would at least make that experience as superlative as possible.

"Stop it at once," commanded her mother. "It's mortifying."

Philippa moved one more plushly upholstered bergère a quarter inch closer to the unlit fireplace before lacing her fingers together and standing perfectly still.

With luck, that would be the end of it.

It was not the end of it.

"If you had done your duty," Mother said, "you would not be rearranging your poor mother's furniture, but rather the Duke of Faircliffe's."

"Wouldn't that be conduct unbecoming a lady?" Philippa murmured.

"A duchess," Mother snapped. "You were to be a *duchess*."

Philippa rather thought the point remained.

Mother pursed her lips. "You should not have attended his gala last week."

"You gave me no choice," Philippa reminded her. "You said, 'Everyone who is anyone will be there, and we are someone.' You readied the carriage and forced Father to come with us."

"Faircliffe is a duke," Mother said, as though Philippa might have forgotten this fact in the past three seconds. "One doesn't decline the invitation of a *duke*, even if he should have married *you* and not that horrible Wynchester orphan—"

"Her name is Chloe," Philippa corrected. "Or 'Her Grace, the Duchess of Faircliffe' to you."

Mother's face empurpled at the injustice.

"And she'll be here at any moment," Philippa added helpfully. "Do you want to greet guests at the door with me?"

This was an olive branch. Mother *adored* hovering at the butler's shoulder and leaping past him to greet each guest, particularly when they were Ladies of Importance and Good Standing.

"I wanted to greet the guests," Mother said, "at your *wedding breakfast*."

Philippa sighed.

Marrying the Duke of Faircliffe was the last thing Philippa had wished to do. Chloe had provided an invaluable service to all parties by drawing his attention elsewhere.

Chloe had *wanted* to marry the duke. Philippa did not. Why couldn't wanting to be with someone—or not—be reason enough?

"He was the greatest catch you were ever likely to get," Mother said. She'd been espousing variations on this theme several times a day, ever since the betrothal fell apart two months ago. "Especially now that you're *old*."

"I'm three and twenty," Philippa reminded her.

Her mother shuddered as though such a high number had never before been achieved by an unmarried woman.

"Now look what you've done," said her mother. "There won't be any more offers."

"I receive half a dozen marriage proposals every season," Philippa reminded her. "I could be ninety years old and they'd still come in. I've a very attractive dowry."

"*Viable* offers," her mother corrected impatiently. "I told you: a title or nothing. And we almost had the highest title of the entire peerage."

Philippa slid her gaze to the clock in the corner of the parlor. A quarter to three. Why, oh why, couldn't her friends be early, today of all days?

"Perhaps if you would've told him your deepest dream was to one day become a duchess," Mother said.

If Philippa had said that, she *would* be married now.

It was the reason she hadn't said it.

"Why would I say something I didn't mean?" she asked reasonably.

"It's how things are done," her mother snapped. "It's called 'flirting.' I'm not saying you must *simper*..."

"I shall not simper."

"But if you *did*," Mother continued, "a little simpering could go a long way."

The faint sound of carriage wheels crunching to a

halt drifted through the open window, followed by eager voices.

Philippa's friends were here.

Thank God.

"If you'll excuse me." She tried to edge past her mother.

Mother didn't budge.

"When I wanted you to be a diamond of the first water, I didn't mean 'cold' and 'hard.'" Mother crossed her arms. "The only things you seem excited about are your books and your little reading circle."

Philippa nodded. "Yes."

"Perhaps you shouldn't have it," Mother mused. "Perhaps the use of my parlor for such bluestocking nonsense shall depend on you marrying the gentleman of my choice."

"An illogical proposition," Philippa said. "If I marry, I'll no longer have need of your parlor. The guests are arriving, Mother. Please let me pass."

"I suppose you're expecting me to preside over a formal tea," Mother said with a sniff.

Philippa was indeed expecting this. Mother insisted that hosting a formal tea after each reading circle made a gathering of bluestockings acceptable.

Every week without fail, her mother burst into the parlor and interrupted some utterly fascinating observation to demand they cease their prattle at once and reconvene in the far less comfortable dining room chairs, crowded about a long table. At which point, they could no longer see and hear one another.

Philippa and her friends much preferred a tray of biscuits and a bottle of wine in the open parlor.

"Lady Eunice," came the butler's deep voice from down the corridor.

"Lady Eunice is here," Philippa whispered. "An *actual lady*."

Mother scrunched her features together, then dashed down the corridor to the front door.

"Lady Eunice," she squealed. "What an honor to have *you* in our humble home once again."

If Philippa were to marry some ton gentleman, Lady Eunice would cease gracing the York residence with her presence every Thursday.

Perhaps Mother ought to think about *that*.

Philippa strode down the corridor and grinned at Lady Eunice. As usual, her friend's auburn hair was impeccably styled *à la grecque* and her day dress was of the height of fashion. Lady Eunice was doing her best to hold her copy of this month's book selection at an angle at which Philippa's mother could not easily read its title.

The five young ladies bubbling through the door behind Lady Eunice were doing the same thing.

How Philippa adored these witty, clever, irreverent bluestockings! The weekly reading circle was when she was happiest, and whom she was happiest with.

"If you'll follow me, ladies." She gestured for them to follow her.

With minimal muffled giggles, they hurried down the corridor and into their weekly sanctum.

"Oatcakes," Damaris said in delight when she saw the plates on the sideboard. Her dark braid bounced as she hurried to pick up a plate.

"Ooh, Madeira," said Lady Eunice. "Don't mind if I do."

Were they spoiling their appetite for the inevitable tea? Worth it. Wine and cakes were an intrinsic component of any self-respecting reading circle.

Florentia grinned, her brown eyes crinkling above light brown apple cheeks dotted with dark brown freckles. She swatted a black ringlet from her forehead and hurried to join the growing queue.

"Look what I have." Sybil pushed her spectacles up her button nose. The queen of lists and charts, Sybil usually had a new calendar for the group to follow. Today, she held out a book.

Philippa plucked the heavy leather volume from her friend's arms. "Eutropius's *Breviarium historiae Romanae*," she breathed in awe. The gilt embossing was pristine and the ribbons like new. "Which printing is this?"

"1762," Sybil replied.

"Let me know when it's translated into English," said Damaris.

"Or French," said Lady Eunice.

"Or Greek," said Florentia.

"Oh, fine," said Jessica. "I'll read the Latin."

"I'm first." Philippa fought the urge to cradle the gorgeous volume to her chest and placed it reverently on her bookshelf next to her collection of illuminated manuscripts. She handed Sybil an uncut copy of Eliza Haywood's *Love in Excess*. "Fair is fair."

Sybil adjusted her spectacles. Her eyes widened. "My life is complete."

A dozen more ladies poured into the parlor, including Chloe—the new Duchess of Faircliffe—and her brash but delightful Great-Aunt Wynchester.

Chloe placed a large wicker basket atop her usual chair.

"What's in the basket?" Sybil asked.

"Your kitten?" asked Florentia.

"Lemon cakes?" Philippa guessed.

"Champagne?" said Lady Eunice.

"My contribution to our charity endeavor," Chloe said, laughing. She pulled two stacks of slender books from her basket and moved them to a side table. "We brought new books for the children's library."

"*And* lemon cakes," announced Great-Aunt Wynchester. The handsome, white-haired older woman passed around a small parcel with more than enough for everyone.

"We should name ourselves the Lemon Cake Ladies," said Damaris as she accepted a cake.

"We're not naming ourselves," Philippa reminded

her. "We're an informal group of friends, not some stuffy society of proper young ladies."

"We're definitely improper young ladies," Lady Eunice agreed. She held up her copy of *Les Liaisons dangereuses*, this month's literary selection.

"How about the Extremely Improper Book Club?" suggested Sybil.

"No," said Philippa.

"Too many words," agreed Chloe.

"How about *Les dangereuses* Ladies?" asked Florentia.

"Grammatically incorrect," said Lady Eunice. "We'd be *Les dames dangereuses*. Or just *Les dangereuses*."

"French is pretentious," Damaris said. "How about... The Unholy Bluestocking Alliance?"

"I forbid the naming of our club," Philippa said. "It's *my* club."

"See?" Sybil glanced up from her new book. "It *is* a club."

Oh, very well, it *was*... for now.

But Philippa could not bear to name her group of cherished friends. A title was too official. It would hurt even more to lose them because her mother deemed bluestockings inappropriate.

"We're a reading circle," she said firmly. "Are we ready to discuss this month's highly anticipated literary masterpiece?"

"Not yet." Chloe glanced about the room with a frown. "Where's Gracie?"

"Gracie is always late," said Damaris.

"Maybe she's with her sister," Lady Eunice said. "Theodosia rarely wishes to attend the reading circle."

That was true. Proper Theodosia always devised wholesome plans to lure Gracie away from improper company. Philippa tried not to be envious at the thought of having a sister who loved her and wanted to spend time with her.

Being an only child could be dull and lonely.

"Wasn't Gracie at the Overton soirée last night?" asked Sybil. "She was probably out until dawn, flirting with ineligible gentlemen."

"Or she's run off with one," Florentia grumbled. "Who does she think she is, Lydia Bennet?"

"You're all just jealous," Lady Eunice pronounced. "You would switch slippers with Gracie in a second if it meant kissing a different handsome rake every night of the week."

Blushes and titters rippled around the room.

Philippa fought a grimace. Kissing a strange man every night did not sound romantic at all.

"There's no sign of Miss Kimball," came a miffed voice from the doorway.

Philippa's mother had poked her head into the room with timing suspicious enough to indicate she'd been listening at the keyhole.

"Wait by the front door," Philippa told her. "She'll be here."

"Of course she will," Mother said with a sniff.

"She has poor manners and no prospects. Insincere attentions from profligate men and communal pity from you lot is the best she can—"

"*Mother*. That's enough." Philippa rose to her feet and crossed to the door. "Conduct *very* unbecoming a lady, Mrs. York. I am certain a hostess as fine as yourself would not slander her guests with idle gossip."

"She stole your betrothed," Mother said peevishly.

"I preemptively jilted my betrothed," Philippa reminded her.

Mother wasn't listening. Her eyes narrowed on Chloe. Mother dropped her voice to a whisper. "If she weren't a duchess, I would not host her for tea. In fact, perhaps I won't host tea for your little group ever again. Don't think I haven't noticed some of them bringing their own cakes. Highly improper. *Very* rude. *Our* chef is French, and I'll have you know that in most of *their* kitchens—"

"Very well," Philippa interrupted. "I understand and respect your wish to withhold formal tea from us for a full month as punishment. I shall inform the others of our loss."

"They'll rue their ways," Mother said with satisfaction. "Just watch."

Philippa closed the door and shoved a handkerchief in the keyhole.

A month. She'd bought a month.

For as long as Mother believed herself to be

punishing Philippa for her choices, the reading circle would remain intact.

She turned to face the group.

They were all watching her, wide-eyed.

"My apologies," Philippa said, her body stiff. "Although not always evident to the eye, my mother is very concerned about impropriety and proper manners. She thinks I don't have any."

"No," Chloe said softly. "She thinks *I* haven't any."

Ah.

Mother's voice had carried.

Wonderful.

"You are not the problem," Philippa said firmly. "I never wanted your husband."

"Philippa never wants any of her suitors," Damaris said. "She's had more offers than all the rest of us combined."

Technically, it was Philippa's parents who had politely refused all of those offers, often before Philippa was even aware of the man's interest. She would bristle at their presumption if she'd had any interest in pursuing the suit. As it was, she much preferred the freedoms of spinsterhood.

"She's unlucky in love," said Lady Eunice.

Florentia sighed. "Poor Philippa."

Philippa clenched her teeth. She was *not* unlucky in love. She was very, very lucky. She had no desire to marry a man whose only interest in her was her dowry, and thus far she had managed to avoid that fate.

She was not swayed by dukes or earls. Indeed, no ton gentleman had ever captured her attention. She had dreaded her wedding day from the moment of her come-out.

Philippa *enjoyed* being single. She didn't want to wed.

She also liked blustery Great-Aunt Wynchester and her niece Chloe, who had inadvertently saved Philippa from a deeply unhappy marriage.

She would turn the topic to their felicitous union instead. Perhaps that would settle any high emotions.

Philippa took the seat next to Chloe to show that all was well and normal.

"How *did* the two of you meet?" she asked with curiosity.

"Oh, the usual way." Chloe's mouth curved into a smile. "I stole his carriage while he was inside of it."

The door to the parlor swung open and Gracie burst inside, her pretty face distraught.

"I need your help!"

CHAPTER 2

Philippa and the other ladies leapt to their feet at once.

"Are you injured?" Philippa hurried to Gracie's side. "What happened?"

"Last night," Gracie said, her breath hitching, "at the Overton soirée, I slipped out to the garden for a moment alone with Lord Rotherham—"

"The notorious rake?" asked Damaris.

"Of course the notorious rake," said Florentia. "Gracie's been angling for a kiss all season."

Sybil straightened with interest. "Did you get one?"

"The kiss isn't the point," Gracie said. "I lost my *hairpin*."

The ladies looked at each other.

"You lost... your hairpin?" Lady Eunice repeated.

Gracie let out a sigh. "Very well, it wasn't *my* hairpin. Which is why I cannot lose it! It's very singular. It's part of a set of twin silver cornflower aigrettes—"

Florentia pointed to a silver flower in her hair. "We *all* have cornflower aigrettes."

"I don't have one," said Sybil.

"Well, now I'm missing one, too," Gracie said impatiently. "Silver, with a row of diamonds down the middle."

"I remember that hairpin," said Damaris. "The diamonds sparkle gloriously in candlelight."

Gracie turned to Chloe. "You must help me. If even half of what I've heard about your family is true..."

"To make certain I'm following," Chloe said. "Last night, you sneaked out of the Overtons' party to exchange kisses in a private garden with a known rake, and in doing so lost a fashionable, *expensive*, diamond-studded silver cornflower hairpin that doesn't belong to you."

Gracie winced. "Your version makes me sound flighty."

Sybil closed her eyes and murmured, "Does it?"

"But it gets worse," Gracie added miserably. "I didn't realize the hairpin was gone until I returned home and my lady's maid remarked on its absence. That was when I remembered Rotherham caressing my head."

"You forgot a rake had caressed your head?"

"She wanted a *kiss*, not a skull massage."

"It was inelegant," Gracie explained. "At one point,

my hair tugged, and he apologized profusely. I thought him clumsy, not cruel. He's meant to be a shameless rake, not a shameless *robber*."

"Anyone would have assumed the same," Sybil assured her.

"I wanted to believe it was an accident, and that the hairpin had fallen without either of us noticing. At first light, my maid and I took a hackney to the Overtons' before my parents awoke—"

"In daylight?" Florentia covered her face with her hand.

"We took every precaution not to be seen," Gracie said quickly. "No one but servants rise before noon."

"I wake at nine," said Sybil.

"In any case," said Gracie, "the section of the garden Rotherham and I were in isn't visible from the house, which is why we chose it. My maid and I spent an hour inspecting leaves and combing through every blade of grass. No sign of the hairpin anywhere. We were forced to return home empty-handed. And now... people *know*."

Philippa blinked. "Who knows?"

"*What* do they know?" asked Chloe.

"*How* can they know," added Florentia, "if you've just said no one saw you?"

"*I* don't know." Gracie dug in her reticule for a wrinkled square of newspaper and shoved it in Philippa's direction. "But this morning's scandal column contained *this*."

Everyone crowded around Philippa.

"'Another conquest for Lord R—'" she read aloud. "'Is another maiden deflower'd? Or is her pin all she's lost?'"

The reading circle gaped at Gracie in horror.

"I know," she said. "*I know.*"

"You said the kiss wasn't important," said Sybil.

"The kiss *isn't* important," Gracie answered. "The *hairpin* is important. It implies we had a private moment. To society, suspicion is as good as proof."

"*Is* it suspicious?" Lady Eunice asked. "If cornflower aigrettes are everywhere, why would anyone think it belonged to you, specifically?"

"Other than Damaris recognizing the hairpin by description alone?" asked Philippa.

"Other than Gracie *always* sneaking off to let her newest swain steal a kiss?" asked Florentia.

"She's not been caught," Sybil reminded her. "Rumors aren't proof."

"Obviously Gracie ought not to use the matching hairpin anymore," Damaris said. "But unless Rotherham wears it about like a trophy, how would someone link the two without witnessing their stolen kiss?"

"Unless he printed this himself, someone *did* see them," Philippa reminded her. She lifted the torn square from the scandal column. "But who? And how?"

Gracie rubbed her face. "I don't know."

"Perhaps your location *was* visible from the house," Florentia suggested.

Gracie shook her head. "We were behind a hedge, beneath the new moon. The diamonds wouldn't even have sparkled."

"Mayhap a servant was outside," suggested Damaris. "A gardener?"

"At one o'clock in the morning on a moonless night?" Gracie said.

"Then Rotherham must have told someone," said Lady Eunice. "The blackguard."

"He would never," Sybil said. "As a rake, he has a reputation for ducking behind the closest folding screen with anything in a skirt. But Rotherham has always been careful to be discreet, lest he compromise one of his conquests and be forced to the altar."

"The point is what will happen if the gossips keep talking," Gracie said desperately. "Like Damaris, my entire family would recognize that hairpin from description alone. I cannot leave Rotherham with evidence of anything. We need to get the hairpin *back*."

Sybil poured Gracie a glass of Madeira. "Whether rakes have any business raking is debatable, but he ought not to be stealing anything more than a kiss."

"Of course you're right," said Florentia. "I am sorry for teasing you, Gracie. I did not realize how serious this was."

"You still don't," Gracie said. "I've not confessed the worst part."

"Wait," Philippa said. "How could your entire

family recognize the description of a pin that doesn't belong to you?"

Gracie hung her head. "Because it belongs to my sister."

Lady Eunice gasped. "You lost *Theodosia's* hairpin?"

"She didn't lose it," Sybil pointed out. "Rotherham stole it."

"Mayhap he'll return it," Damaris suggested.

"He won't," Gracie said. "It may be unwise, but as soon as I saw the scandal column, I sent a letter."

"Unwise," Florentia said, "but understandable."

"Did he respond?" Philippa asked.

Gracie opened her reticule and handed Philippa a folded square.

"'I've no recollection of any garden,'" she read aloud, "'and I suggest you forget it as well.'"

"I cannot 'forget,'" said Gracie. "Theodosia and I were born one year apart on the same day. The matching hairpins were a gift from our late grandmother. Mine is inscribed with a 'G' and the year of my birth. Theodosia's is engraved with a 'T' and the year of hers. If the details of the missing pin get published..."

"Theodosia could lose her reputation, through no fault of her own," Sybil finished bleakly.

"Not her reputation," Gracie said, her face pale. "Theodosia's *beau*. Mr. Voss is a parson and very proper. Theodosia adores him. Theirs is a love match. The first banns are to be read a week from Sunday."

Damaris winced. "A public humiliation would be more than enough to ruin her."

"It wouldn't even be necessary." Gracie closed her eyes. "If Mr. Voss believes Theodosia to be unfaithful, he'll call off the marriage himself."

Lady Eunice looked bewildered. "Why would Rotherham do this?"

"I don't know," Gracie answered. "I've done nothing to cross him."

"Perhaps he took it as security that you would not confess to being alone with him. He could plant the pin anywhere he liked and ruin you without ruining himself."

"I wasn't *going* to tell anyone," Gracie said. "I wanted a kiss, not a compromise, or I could have screamed for witnesses right there in the garden. He needn't steal my sister's pin."

"What did Theodosia say?" Philippa asked softly.

Gracie looked horrified. "I didn't tell her. I *can't* tell her." She turned to Chloe. "I must get the pin back from Rotherham before she notices it missing. Or someone else realizes it belongs to her."

"Not just returned safely," Lady Eunice said. "Returned and strutted about conspicuously. If you and your sister are seen wearing both aigrettes, then it cannot be the alleged hairpin mentioned in the scandal column."

"But how?" Damaris's eyes were wide. "He won't

admit to stealing kisses from Gracie, much less pocketing her pin."

"Seems simple to me," Great-Aunt Wynchester announced. "If he won't give it back... then we take it from him."

"Steal a stolen hairpin?" Sybil scoffed. "From wherever he's hidden it? That's impossible."

"Well," said Chloe, "I wouldn't say *impossible*."

"It's definitely impossible," said Lady Eunice. "He and his brother live alone and host no parties. A lady would lose her reputation by calling upon such a domicile, not that Rotherham would allow Gracie inside to root through his belongings."

"Of course he would try to prevent her from doing so," said Great-Aunt Wynchester. Her crafty smile deepened the wrinkles about her dark, pretty eyes. "If he *knew* about it."

"Sneak *into* a bachelor residence?" Damaris squeaked. "That's *definitely* impossible."

"Well," said Chloe. "I may know a few people who have done so."

Florentia arched a brow. "Like who, for example?"

"Like me," Great-Aunt Wynchester declared. "And any Wynchester worth his or her salt."

"It *is* true. Thank the stars." Gracie clasped her hands to her chest. "Rumor has it your family helps those who have no other recourse. That when all hope is lost, you somehow find a way."

"Idle gossip," Florentia scolded her. "No one can possibly achieve all of the things the Wynchesters are rumored to be able to do." She paused and turned to Chloe. "Can you?"

"I don't know what cases we're rumored to have solved," Chloe hedged.

"But yes," barked Great-Aunt Wynchester. "All of that and more. Obviously we can retrieve a *hairpin*."

Gracie clapped her hands. "If you do, you'll save my life *and* my sister's wedding!"

Philippa's gaze met Great-Aunt Wynchester's. The older woman's eyes crinkled for only a moment before the others crowded around the Wynchesters, bubbling over with questions.

"Did you really track down that debutante's missing fiancé?"

Chloe inspected her fingernails. "We might have."

"You really sneaked food and medicine into Coldbath Fields Prison?"

Chloe grinned. "Guilty."

"What about the weaving factory incident with the bats?"

Great-Aunt Wynchester patted her white hair. "Definitely us."

Philippa gazed at them in wonder. Being a Wynchester was *so* much better than being a proper young lady. How Philippa wished she had cases to solve and daring rescues to perform, rather than handkerchiefs to embroider and dinner parties to endure!

"I'll pay you anything you ask," said Gracie.

"We don't want your money," Chloe replied warmly. "You're our friend."

"What we need is time to devise a plan," Damaris said.

"It's Thursday afternoon," Florentia reminded them. "We only have nine and a half days before the first banns are read."

CHAPTER 3

"Take your seat, Gracie," commanded Great-Aunt Wynchester.

Gracie wrung her hands. "I'm too upset to talk about books."

"No one is talking about books," Philippa assured her. "The Wynchesters are going to discuss your case."

"And *then* we'll talk about books," said Sybil.

Philippa placed a chair in front of the parlor door to keep it closed, and verified her handkerchief was stuffed fully inside the keyhole.

"Don't worry," said Great-Aunt Wynchester. "We won't discuss legally questionable maneuvers under this roof."

Philippa wished she could be wherever the legally questionable adventures were had.

"The first question," said Chloe, "is whether Lord Rotherham is in possession of the hairpin."

Gracie frowned. "The gossip column clearly states—"

"We know what it *says*," Philippa said slowly. "Whoever wrote this either saw or was informed what had happened. We don't know which, and we don't know what happened afterwards."

"Very good," said Great-Aunt Wynchester. "That's exactly it."

Philippa flushed.

"All right, then." Chloe fished in her wicker basket and pulled out a leather-bound notebook and a pencil. "Where are the places the hairpin *could* be?"

"His rented rooms," said Gracie.

"And where is that?"

The ladies exchanged blank glances.

"Brook Street?" Lady Eunice said.

"Don't worry." Chloe made a note. "His precise direction is simple enough to ascertain. Where else might the pin be?"

"On his person," said Lady Eunice. "He might be wearing it pinned to his lapel."

"We'll inspect every inch of his clothing," said Chloe. "Where else?"

"He could have sold it," Damaris suggested.

Gracie groaned and dropped her head in her hands.

"Pawn shops," Chloe murmured as her pencil flew across the page. "Fences..."

Lady Eunice blinked. "Fences?"

"A receiver of stolen goods," Great-Aunt Wynchester explained.

"Would Lord Rotherham know such an individual?" Florentia asked doubtfully. "Or risk being seen connected to such?"

"He could send a servant," Sybil pointed out. "Or wear a disguise."

Gracie moaned even louder.

"Don't worry," said Chloe. "We'll check."

"You'll... investigate an unknown quantity of indeterminate businesses, both above-ground and underground, to determine if their unknown proprietors have transacted with an equally unknown intermediary?" Lady Eunice asked politely.

"She'll have her brother do it," said Great-Aunt Wynchester. "He might already know the answer. He reads the scandal columns, too."

"In the meantime," Chloe said, "we'll concentrate on recouping the lost item from the two most likely locations."

Damaris blinked. "Stealing it from his lodgings or his person?"

"Shh," Sybil hissed. "This isn't where we discuss maneuvers of questionable legality."

"I'm not certain 'questionable' is the right word," Florentia murmured.

"We could do," Philippa said. "What if we plotted our stratagems in Latin? No one in this house would understand if they overheard."

Sybil clapped her hands. "*Perfectus!*"

"Why is it always Latin?" Florentia asked, her translation stilted but understandable. "Why not Greek?"

"I'm dreadful with the Classics," said Gracie in tortured Greek. "Cannot our secret language be something modern, such as Italian or French?"

"French isn't *secret*," Damaris responded in Italian. "The entire beau monde speaks French."

"*Ma mère ne peut pas*," Philippa said. *My mother cannot.* "She arranged tutors for me, but her vocabulary is limited to naming desserts and a handful of sauces."

Chloe and her Great-Aunt Wynchester exchanged an unreadable look.

"I'm so sorry," Philippa said in English, her ears heating in embarrassment. "Of course you two are the most important people to be included in the conversation. We bluestockings are always trying to outdo each other with knowledge, and it didn't occur to me to ask—"

"*Le français est parfait*," Chloe assured her.

"Much better than Greek," Great-Aunt Wynchester added in halting Latin.

Florentia's eyes widened.

"We appreciate your initial assumption that we *could*, rather than that we could not," Chloe said with a smile. Her French accent was passable. "To be honest, our Latin is middling and I cannot speak a word of Greek."

"So there *is* something the infamous Wynchesters

cannot do," Sybil breathed.

"They need us," Florentia crowed. "I'm excellent at Greek."

"They don't need us," Gracie said. "My sister's hairpin has nothing to do with Greek. Can we please talk about how to save her reputation and her betrothal?"

"Don't worry," said Chloe. "I have a plan."

"We'd best put it into motion quickly," said Lady Eunice. "Not only because the first banns will be read in nine days, but because the season is over. The ton will retire to their country estates or go on holiday. Many have left already. Lord Rotherham could disappear at any moment."

"All true." Chloe slid her notebook into her basket and pushed to her feet. "Come along, Aunt. There isn't a moment to waste."

"*Now* we'll talk about books," Sybil said with satisfaction. She held up her set of *Les Liaisons dangereuses*. "This was a deuced good one."

"Part Two was a disappointment, and the author failed to foreshadow the development in Part Three," Gracie snapped. "There. We've discussed it. I cannot read another word about dangerous liaisons when all I can think about is how my sister will never forgive me for ruining her life along with mine."

"Come with us," said Chloe. "We'll accompany you home, and we can go over the details again along the way."

"Thank you," Gracie said gratefully.

Philippa hastened to move the chair and unblock the door.

Once Gracie and the Wynchesters had gone, Florentia said hopefully, "May we speak Greek now?"

"We should create a schedule," Sybil said. "A different language every week would be fair."

"You and your schedules," Florentia grumbled.

"You're just bitter because you picked the monthly book twice as often as anyone else until Sybil started a rotation," Lady Eunice said.

"Put Greek last," Damaris whispered. "Cheaters deserve to wait."

Florentia huffed.

Sybil twisted her hands in her lap. "Poor Gracie, and poor Theodosia, who doesn't even know her reputation is at risk! No wonder Gracie is frantic. She and her sister are so close, they're practically twins. Something like this could cause lasting damage to their relationship."

"We'll do everything in our power to help Gracie," Lady Eunice said. "Our reading circle is a sisterhood, too."

"That's right." Damaris lifted her fist in the air. "No one bests the Ladies' Literature Club!"

"We are not the Ladies' Literature Club," Philippa murmured.

Lady Eunice tilted her head. "Do you think the Wynchesters will recover the hairpin?"

"I hope so," Philippa admitted. "They're our best chance."

"Our *only* chance," Damaris said. "It's not as though Gracie can go to the Runners or publicly shame Lord Rotherham for his behavior without destroying her own reputation in the process."

"And then she'd no longer be welcome in the Lusty Literary Ladies Society," Sybil said sadly.

"We wouldn't expel her from the League of Lusty Ladies over a ruined reputation," said Lady Eunice.

"It's not a league," said Philippa, "and we wouldn't have to. My mother wouldn't allow her across our threshold."

More likely, Mother would disband Philippa's group altogether.

Her stomach sickened at the idea of losing this cherished sisterhood. The only time she felt comfortable in her own home—in her own skin—was here in her private parlor during the Thursday afternoon reading circle.

"Aha!" Mother appeared in the open doorway as though conjured directly from Philippa's unhappy thoughts. "Coming out of your cave, are you? Well, there's no tea today, and you've Philippa to thank for that. Come along, then. I'll bid you adieu at the door."

Sybil sent stricken eyes toward Philippa.

"We didn't even discuss the book," she whispered.

"Next time," Philippa promised her, and hoped it was true. "I'll do everything in my power to discuss literature with you as often and for as long as I can."

Lady Eunice frowned. "That sounds as though you're unsure how long—"

"Tut, tut," said Philippa's mother, clapping her hands as though to startle mice. "That's enough Bluestocking Club for one day."

Philippa clenched her fists. "We're not—"

But it was too late. Her mother was shepherding every one of the ladies down the corridor and out through the front door.

"That was rude," Philippa informed her when the last guest was gone.

"Was it?" Mother answered. "As rude as jilting a duke?"

"I didn't *jilt* him... exactly," Philippa muttered. It was more a mutual jilting.

"We'll burn your books," her mother said, as though commenting upon the weather. "Starting with your precious illuminated manuscripts."

"*What?*" Philippa burst out. "Why?"

Mother smirked. "You can stop it from happening, if you like."

"Of course I want to stop that from happening," Philippa sputtered. "How do I stop it from happening?"

"Marry the man your father chooses for you," Mother replied. "No chicanery this time."

Philippa's chest felt leaden and hollow. No more mutual jilting. This time, she would have to go through with it.

"Has he selected the groom?" she asked dully.

"Not yet. We're looking for a respectable lord proud enough not to allow his wife to mix with riffraff," Mother said with a sniff.

How sweet.

"You never used to hate my friends," Philippa said.

"That was before you invited a Wynchester into our midst," Mother replied. "If she weren't a duchess, I'd toss her out into the street."

Philippa clenched her teeth. Chloe and her Great-Aunt Wynchester fit in perfectly with the others. It felt as though they'd been part of the reading circle all along.

"Enjoy your bluestocking nonsense whilst you have it," Mother said. "Your husband won't be as indulgent as I have been."

She strode off without awaiting a response.

Philippa's stomach twisted.

Soon, her Thursday afternoon respite would be gone.

CHAPTER 4

"Thank you," Gracie said a few hours later as she climbed into the Yorks' carriage.

Philippa moved herself and her voluminous lace skirts closer to the window to create room.

Gracie flopped onto the squab and rubbed her wan face.

"My parents informed me in no uncertain terms that Chloe and her aunt walking me home for two hundred yards was on the very edge of respectability, and that was only because Chloe is now the Duchess of Faircliffe. Accepting an invitation to the Wynchester residence in Islington is completely out of the question. So I told them my dear friend Miss York had invited me button shopping."

"Then we must purchase a few buttons on the return journey," Philippa said.

She had told *her* family she was visiting Gracie, who had been feeling out of sorts... but neglected to mention where, precisely, the visiting would take place.

"Have you been to the Wynchesters' house before?" Gracie asked.

"I have not," Philippa replied, unable to tamp down a renewed frisson of excitement.

She had long wanted to see how the Wynchesters lived, but had never dreamt of being invited inside their home.

Technically, she *still* had not.

Gracie had been invited, and Philippa's carriage was the Trojan horse allowing the visit to occur.

"What do you suppose they want to know that I haven't already told them?" Gracie asked.

"Didn't you ask?"

Gracie shook her head. "There was no time. Theodosia met me on the front path and Chloe and I had to pretend we were admiring the fine June weather."

"Hasn't your sister wondered why you haven't returned her hairpin?"

A guilty look flashed across Gracie's face.

"She doesn't know it's gone," Gracie admitted. "I borrowed her diamond hairpin without her knowledge. She rarely attends parties, and my hair looks ever so much better with two pins."

"Oh, Gracie," Philippa said.

"We always borrow each other's things without asking," Gracie protested. "I imagine a dozen items from my dressing room currently reside in hers. I had planned to put the pin back in her jewelry box as soon as I returned from the soirée. I didn't expect it to be *stolen*. Or described salaciously in a gossip column."

"No, I suppose one wouldn't expect that," Philippa murmured.

Her mind was not on the theft, but rather how lovely it must be to have a sister. Someone to share wardrobes with. Someone to *talk* to. The closest thing she had to sisterhood was the reading circle.

Philippa loved her books more than anything, but that was in part because books were all she had. Her heart had room for so much more. If not a robust family life, then at least a spot of fun from time to time.

Gracie's mouth fell open, and she placed her fingertips to the window. "Is *that*... where the 'poor orphans' live? I'd read the gossip, but I had no idea..."

Philippa peered over Gracie's shoulder as the carriage turned down a long driveway.

For once, the gossips had spoken true. The Wynchester property was more than twice the size of any self-respecting London square. A thick hedgerow delineated its boundary from its neighbors, and a magnificent three-story home rose in the center, complete with white fluted columns and a dizzying array of tall, sparkling windows.

"How lucky they are," Gracie breathed. "I suppose this *was* Baron Vanderbean's residence."

"It still is," Philippa reminded her. "His son inherited the property as well as the title."

"Have you seen the new baron?" Gracie asked.

Philippa shook her head. "Have you?"

"I never even saw the old baron," Gracie admitted. "My father did, once, many years ago. Papa says the baron was all that was correct and kind, but dashed reclusive. I suppose the new baron must be the same way."

"I wonder," said Philippa. "What made your father think the prior baron was a recluse? Did he refuse to return your father's calls?"

Gracie's eyes widened. "My family would *never* call upon a Wynchester."

"I suspect the same is true of the rest of the beau monde," Philippa said dryly.

Gracie made a face. "Perhaps Baron Vanderbean was not reclusive so much as... lonely?"

"I'm uncertain how lonely one could be with a house full of Wynchesters," Philippa pointed out. "Every gossip column claims a different quantity of them—anywhere from ten to twenty. Besides, Chloe has friends. I'm sure the others do, too. It is 'Polite Society' who has lost an opportunity."

"Don't let your mother hear you saying that," Gracie whispered.

"Oh, I know," Philippa said with a sigh. "I know."

If her parents learned she had gone to Islington with Gracie... But what did it matter? Soon Philippa's parents would foist a suitor upon her, and freedom as she knew it would be gone for ever.

This might well be her last chance for adventure.

The carriage pulled to a stop in front of the door. The York tiger in his sharp green livery handed the ladies down.

A kindly looking butler opened the front door. "Follow me, if you please."

"Don't you require our calling cards?" Gracie stammered.

The butler's eyes crinkled. "Miss Gracie Kimball and Miss Philippa York, I presume?"

Philippa had to stop herself from curtseying.

"How did he know you would come with me?" Gracie whispered.

Philippa had no idea. "I imagine the Wynchesters know far more than they are given credit for."

Once they had dispensed with their hats and gloves, the butler led the ladies out of the luxurious antechamber, past an opulent marble staircase, and down a silk-lined corridor to an absolutely gorgeous sitting room filled with comfortable chairs and sofas, and awash with light from several large bay windows complete with thick cushions and fluffy pillows.

"What a beautiful room." Philippa gazed about in wonder. "Any of those windows would create a truly spectacular reading nook."

"You're right." Chloe entered behind them and pointed toward a particularly inviting window. "That was my favorite reading nook, when I still lived here. I'm afraid my beloved cushion has fallen into disuse. You're welcome to it whenever you please."

How Philippa *wished* she could accept such an offer!

"Thank you, Mr. Randall," Chloe said to the butler. "If you'll inform the others—"

But there was no need. Wynchester siblings poured into the room.

First came a tall gentleman with golden skin, a head of dark curls, and a boyish grin he couldn't quite repress.

"My brother Graham," Chloe said.

Next was a plump, pretty woman with mischievous eyes and a heavy cane with a handle shaped like a serpent.

"My sister Elizabeth."

Next was a handsome gentleman with rich brown skin, cropped black curly hair, and what appeared to be some sort of... monkey-badger? ...nibbling upon his cravat.

"My brother Jacob."

Last came an ethereal wisp of a girl, even shorter than Philippa herself, and perhaps weighing half as much. A spot of celestial blue paint marred the tip of her dainty nose.

"And my sister Marjorie. Family, this is Miss York and Miss Kimball."

"I would be honored if you all called me Philippa."

Was that too forward? It was definitely too forward.

But *oh*, how she would adore being friends with this family! If ever there was a group of men and women who would not stand stiffly upon pomp and formality, it would be the Wynchesters. It would be like the freedom of her Thursday afternoon reading circle, but all of the time.

Before Chloe joined the group, Philippa hadn't thought much about Wynchesters. She knew they existed—there was plenty of gossip and tall tales that might not be fiction after all—but since they weren't part of the beau monde, she'd never actually met a Wynchester in person until this past year.

Now, she couldn't imagine life without Chloe and her great-aunt, whose irreverent commentary was always a highlight of Philippa's week. She didn't just want to be *like* Great-Aunt Wynchester as she grew older. Philippa hoped to be friends *with* her, and the rest of her fearless family.

"Philippa, then," said Graham, and lifted her fingers to his lips.

"Don't let Tommy see you do that," whispered Jacob's... monkey-badger?

Graham grinned. "I'd like to see Tommy do something about it."

Philippa froze. The Wynchesters weren't *matchmaking*, were they?

"What I'd like to see us do," Chloe said firmly, "is to prevent a disaster from befalling Miss Kimball's sister. Marjorie, if you'd take Gracie to your studio?"

The blond waif nodded eagerly and motioned for Gracie to follow.

Philippa took a step after them.

"Oh, they'll be fine," said Chloe. "Stay here with us."

There was no doubt Gracie would be fine. Philippa hadn't followed out of an instinct to chaperone, but because she was dying to see more of the Wynchesters' extraordinary home... and meet the rest of the Wynchesters.

Horace Wynchester—the new Baron Vanderbean—must be here somewhere, as well as a Tommy, the elderly Great-Aunt Wynchester, and any number of other relatives. Didn't the new baron have a sister? Honoria, maybe?

No wonder this family was more effective than the Bow Street Runners. The Wynchesters outnumbered them, two to one.

"Come and sit," said Chloe, ushering everyone toward a crescent of comfortable sofas before a marble fireplace.

Philippa took a seat on the sofa closest to the windows. It put her back toward the Wynchesters' stupendous garden but gave her the best view of the open sitting-room door, lest any new Wynchesters stroll down the corridor.

Graham, Jacob, and Jacob's monkey-badger took the sofa opposite. Elizabeth and Chloe took the sofa at a right angle, facing the fireplace, with Chloe seated closest to Philippa.

"Are we waiting for someone?" she asked.

The siblings exchanged glances again.

"Like who?" Graham asked.

"I don't know," Philippa said uncertainly. Who was likely to share a sofa with her? "Great-Aunt Wynchester, mayhap? Or..." She gripped her lace skirts. They *were* matchmaking. Perhaps they would find a better match than Philippa's parents. "Is it... Baron Vanderbean?"

"It is not Baron Vanderbean," Chloe said.

"*Probably* not Baron Vanderbean," Elizabeth amended. "One can never *guarantee* a lack of Vanderbean. Or anyone else, really."

"Would you like to meet my mongoose?" Jacob asked. "I rescued Orville from an ill-kept menagerie. He knows eight commands and can tackle a viper from ten paces."

"That sounds..." Philippa trailed off. Useful? Useless? Terrifying?

"Always say no," Chloe whispered. "No matter what the animal."

"I liked Tiglet," Philippa whispered back. "I suppose he's your kitten "

Jacob's smile widened. "Tiglet was mine at the time that you met him. I taught him everything he knows."

Philippa frowned. "Does Tiglet know many things?"

"You'd be surprised," Graham murmured.

"Tiglet seems clever," Philippa admitted. "I just hadn't assumed him to be a *trained* kitten. I suppose I noticed—"

The sensation of being watched prickled along her skin. She darted her gaze toward the open door.

A willowy young woman with a profusion of red-brown curls stood just outside of the sitting room. When her startled dark eyes met Philippa's, her cheekbones flushed red, and she disappeared down the corridor.

"Who was that?" Philippa asked. "Was it Honoria?"

The Wynchesters turned to look over their shoulders, but of course no one was there, and the moment was gone.

"It might have been," said Elizabeth.

"Or not," added Graham.

Philippa gazed at the narrow section of corridor she could see from her sofa. It remained stubbornly empty.

"Whilst Marjorie is managing the hairpin," Chloe said, "shall we work out what we know about Lord Rotherham? Philippa, I thought you might help with this part. You must cross paths with him at ton events."

"I suppose so," she said. "He never took much notice of me."

Or she him, if she was being honest.

She was dreadful at recognizing when men were flirting with her, and even worse at flirting back. The reading circle had long despaired of Philippa ever finding The One. Her parents despaired of their daughter finding anyone at all. She hoped their search for a suitor was going just as badly as her own had done.

"For the longest while," she said, "Rotherham had been besotted by Miss Ipsley. I don't know what happened—"

The Wynchesters spun expectant faces toward Graham, who nodded impatiently and waved a hand. They turned back toward Philippa.

"—and, well," she continued once it was clear they weren't going to explain, "after Rotherham's betrothal to Miss Ipsley never materialized, he became quite the rake. He seems to be attempting to out-rake himself with every new escapade. Really, Gracie could tell you more. I've sat at a dinner table with him and partnered for a country-dance or two, but never engaged him in private conversation."

Graham pulled a notebook from his pocket and lifted his eyes to Philippa. "Have you heard much about Rotherham's poetry?"

She stared at him in befuddlement. "Poetry? *Rotherham?*"

"There are many town poetry circles and poet societies," Jacob explained. "I am a member of several, although I rarely attend. My poetry is private."

"But..." Graham prompted.

Jacob stroked his mongoose. "But on one memorable occasion, I attended the same event as Lord Rotherham and his younger brother, Mr. Briggs, who is well known in poetry circles."

"Mr. Briggs is an accomplished poet?" Philippa

said in surprise.

"He said 'well known,'" Graham murmured. "Not 'good.'"

"Briggs's poems are *technically* fine," Jacob said, "but... boring, I suppose. It is as though someone had given him the recipe for how a poem ought to be, and he creates exactly that every time, with nothing of himself in it. At best, he'd throw in an obscure word or two of Latin for spice."

Mr. Briggs and his infernal Latin. Philippa fought the urge to roll her eyes. He had once gently informed Philippa that ladies' brains were too delicate to properly comprehend the declension of adjectives and pronouns.

"And Rotherham?" Chloe asked.

Jacob's eyes brightened. "It was his first time at any poetry circle. Despite the brothers' usual bond, Briggs teased Rotherham to read a poem aloud, clearly not expecting his brother to have any. Lord Rotherham pulled a tightly folded scrap of foolscap from his coat pocket and bowled us over with his poem."

"It was *good?*" Philippa said in disbelief. According to gossip, Rotherham had graduated from Oxford and Eton on charm and good blood alone. Briggs was the brother with the brains.

"Technically, his poem was a disaster," Jacob admitted. "The timing... the rhymes... But, yes, it was wonderful. One of the most haunting, visceral poems I have ever heard. All about pining for a lost love, which you might *think* would be well trodden ground. Rotherham managed to inject so much desperation into each line, it was as though the listener's heart was breaking, too."

"The lost love is Miss Ipsley, I presume?"

"I presume," Jacob agreed. "Rotherham had barely spoken the final words, 'no one shall e'er take her place', when he was whisked upstairs by the hostess of the poetry circle. I've never seen Briggs more livid. It was his turn next, and everyone was too busy chortling and gossiping to pay any attention. He stormed out without another word. Rotherham didn't come back downstairs for an hour."

"So, either he yearns for Miss Ipsley, and none can take her place in his heart..." Elizabeth began.

"...or Rotherham is using the ruse of 'heartbroken swain' to lure softhearted ladies into his rakish web," Chloe finished. "Or both."

"What has poetry to do with the stolen hairpin?" Philippa asked.

"We don't know yet," said Graham. "Maybe something. Maybe nothing. I paid a call and enquired as to his motivations."

"You *asked* Rotherham why he stole Gracie's hairpin?" Philippa said in disbelief.

"Not Gracie," he answered. "The tiara of a Miss Jarvis, the night of Faircliffe's end-of-season gala."

Her mouth dropped open. "Rotherham has done this before?"

"At the time, we weren't certain why he had taken

the tiara, or what he meant to do with it. Money? Retaliation? Nor could we *prove* he'd done so. Miss Jarvis was certain, but not confident enough to bring a legal case against a lord. We were forced to wait and see what happened with the tiara."

"What did happen to it?"

"Nothing," Graham replied simply. "It hasn't been seen since that night. We've kept an eye on him ever since. He wouldn't admit to having purloined the tiara, much less explain why."

"What made you believe he would he tell you anything at all?"

"What people confess to my brother might surprise you," Chloe murmured.

Jacob's eyes sparkled. "There was the lighthouse incident—"

"—and the beekeeper intervention," Chloe said with a smile.

"Don't forget the plumbers' assembly!" Elizabeth doubled over her cane with laughter. "Or the time he was suspended in a bell tower for an hour before dropping in on that poor monk."

"He confessed all," Graham said solemnly. "He also thought I was a ghost."

"Not everything goes so easily," Chloe explained. "Rotherham has strong reasons not to cooperate—"

"Prison, for example," said Elizabeth.

"He has a courtesy title," Jacob reminded her. "Do firstborn sons of lords go to prison?"

Graham set down his book. "Legally, yes. *Prac-*

tically..."

Chloe's lip curled. "Stealing in order to have something to eat is one thing. Robbing a friend for no reason is rude and unacceptable. How it infuriates me that this rake can steal diamonds and face no charges, whereas a child could be imprisoned or sent to the gallows for stealing twelve-pence to feed their family."

"It shall not stand," Graham assured her. "Now we know to look for a pattern. We will stop him."

"The first banns are a week from Sunday," Chloe reminded him. "That gives us nine days."

"What do you know about the sister's intended?" Graham asked Philippa.

"Mr. Voss seems happily betrothed," she replied, "and... very conventional. He and Theodosia both share fairly rigid outlooks on life. If he has any reason to doubt her faithfulness, he won't marry her."

"Causing *her* a lost love," said Jacob.

"Worse," said Chloe. "Causing her to lose all future loves as well. Being a jilt is scandalous, but being *jilted*... No one will court her. They'll think he broke the engagement because she was unfaithful."

There was an uncomfortable beat of silence.

"I was not jilted," Philippa reminded them. "I didn't even technically jilt your husband. I politely rejected his imminent proposal."

The silence did not become less awkward.

Jacob cleared his throat. "We must act quickly. Briggs and his brother shall soon be off on their usual summer tour together. But they'll remove to their country estate for a fortnight first."

"Their *parents'* estate," Graham corrected. "Lord and Lady Strathmore."

"The point stands," Chloe said. "What is Rotherham's schedule for tomorrow?"

Graham flipped through his book. "On Fridays, Rotherham rises between ten and eleven, on average, breaks his fast at home, visits his club for an hour or two, then stops by Berkeley Square for flavored ice before taking a horse to Hyde Park for the obligatory afternoon ton promenade."

Philippa blinked. "How did you collect information that detailed on Lord Rotherham?"

"Everyone knows Rotherham's habits at the park."

"*I* didn't know."

"That's because you never *go* to the park," Graham pointed out.

Jacob chuckled. "Graham has collected detailed information on everyone important in London for more than a decade. He has informants at several grand houses, important organizations, street sweepers and shopkeepers, scandal sheets and newspapers... You should see *your* family's book."

"Do not show Philippa her book," Chloe said.

"Wait," Philippa said. "I have a book?"

"I will investigate how the newspaper acquired this gossip." Graham closed his journal. "Someone must know something. Meanwhile, Rotherham promenades at the fashionable hour without fail, in order to glimpse Miss Ipsley, who no longer opens her door to him."

"Hence his horse?" Chloe asked.

Graham nodded. "Hence, the horse. On foot, Rotherham's pace would be too slow to keep up with her barouche. If he drove his own conveyance, he would be forced to match the speed of the queue. A steed allows him to be nimble."

"But wait," said Philippa. "I demand to see my book. Chloe, you cannot refuse me. It'll be my next reading circle pick. Once it's on Sybil's chart, the selection *must* be honored."

"You do not want the reading circle to read your book," Chloe said.

"I don't?" Philippa straightened. "Do I have secrets?"

"Chloe will oversee Rotherham's flavored ices," said Elizabeth. "Lads, I assume you can breach his residence?"

"No problem," Jacob said. He turned to Graham and whispered, "Where is it?"

Graham flipped through the pages of his book. "Lord Rotherham and Mr. Briggs are renting rooms on 86 Brook Street."

Chloe handed her brothers two folded papers from her basket. "Copies of Tommy's map of the area, annotated with the usual."

Philippa blinked. They had maps of the street where the brothers were renting rooms? Did the Wynchesters have maps of every corner in London?

The men perused the sheets.

"Thorough as ever," Jacob said.

Graham nodded. "This is perfect."

Chloe turned to Elizabeth. "You'll guard the street?"

Elizabeth patted her cane. "It will be my pleasure."

"Splendid." Chloe leaned back. "Now all we need is—"

"She's amazing!" Gracie burst through the open doorway, followed by the ethereal Marjorie. "I showed her my pin, and she made me explain the minute differences in Theodosia's pin over and over, and then she—well, *look!*"

Marjorie held up half a dozen identical, pocket-sized colored drawings of the missing hairpin depicted from various angles.

"It's *exact*," Gracie crowed. "Size and everything. Even the inscription is just so."

"Shall we begin at one o'clock?" Chloe asked.

In unison, her siblings gave a sharp nod. "One o'clock."

"In that case..." She ushered Philippa and Gracie out of the cozy sitting room, past the awe-inspiring marble staircase, and back to the front door. "Thank you so much for coming. Mr. Randall has your bonnets and gloves. Gracie, I'll call on you tomorrow evening with news."

Philippa accepted her hat and gloves in silence.

There was no way she was missing this escapade.

CHAPTER 5

At a quarter to one the following afternoon, Philippa and Gracie exited Philippa's front door, crossed Grosvenor Square, and began a leisurely, casual stroll down Brook Street toward Lord Rotherham's rented apartments.

"I don't want to see him," said Gracie. "If I do, I'll turn into a screeching termagant and make an even bigger scandal out of this mess."

"You won't see him," Philippa reminded her. "He's at Gunter's Tea Shop eating flavored ices, and then he'll ride his horse to Hyde Park for three hours, mooncalfing at his lost love."

Several members of the reading circle bore grudges against Miss Ipsley, who was Fashionable and spent an entire season proclaiming how Completely Unlike Those Unfashionable Bluestockings she was to anyone who would listen—which was most of the ton. Rotherham was *also* Fashionable and shared Miss Ipsley's disdain for books and learning. They were a perfect match, if in a boring way, and Rotherham seemed determined to rewin his lost love's hand.

Gracie bit her lip. "You don't think he'd send her my sister's hairpin as a courtship gift, do you?"

"It would be strange if he did," Philippa answered. "Given it has your sister's birth year and initial engraved on the back."

She supposed any jeweler could smooth over an old inscription in order to etch a new one, but doing so would be certain to raise an eyebrow. Rotherham was well known for his expensive taste in fine horseflesh and men's apparel. He could afford to purchase a trinket for Miss Ipsley if that were his intention. She hoped he would not be cavalier with someone else's possession.

Then again, stranger things had happened.

"There it is," Philippa said. "Number 86."

They stood at the corner on the opposite side of the street.

"What do we do now?" Gracie whispered.

"Observe," Philippa replied.

Gracie bit her lip. "We act natural. Just two young ladies, strolling down an ordinary residential street—"

"We stopped strolling."

"—enjoying a completely unremarkable afternoon constitutional, for a bit of exercise," Gracie finished.

"Again, we're standing still," said Philippa.

Gracie sighed. "Staring at number 86. Conspicuously and unnaturally."

"It's complicated," Philippa admitted. "I've never raided a villain's dwelling before."

"And you won't this time," came Lord Rotherham's voice from right behind them.

Philippa's blood froze.

The color drained from Gracie's shocked face.

Slowly, they turned around to face the wretched thief.

Elizabeth Wynchester gazed back at them. Alone. With an exasperated expression on her face and a heavy serpent-tipped cane beneath one hand.

"What the devil are the two of *you* doing here?" she demanded. "This is a case for the Wynchesters, not the Bullheaded Bluestockings Society."

"That's definitely not the name," Philippa muttered.

"It was *her* idea," said Gracie. "She said you needed us."

Philippa's boot trod ungently upon Gracie's toe.

Elizabeth arched a single brow. No comment was necessary.

"How did you make Rotherham's voice?" Philippa blurted out.

"How did you make Rotherham's voice?" Elizabeth parroted, this time in *Philippa's* voice.

Philippa's mouth fell open.

"I am here as sentry to guard the street," Elizabeth said. "*You* bumblebees shouldn't be here at all."

Gracie frowned. "How can you guard anything? I thought you needed that cane."

Philippa kicked her in the leg.

"I do need this cane," Elizabeth replied. "It helps me walk when my joints won't move. It also conceals a sharp blade, to use when impertinent *interlopers* refuse to move out of my way." She gave them both a pointed look.

"She means us," Gracie whispered.

"I know." Philippa took a breath and faced Elizabeth. "You need us." The Wynchesters did not need her. Philippa needed *them*. She needed adventure. To feel alive, for a little longer, before she wed some stranger. "Gracie can positively identify the hairpin when you find it."

"A mongoose could positively identify the hairpin," Elizabeth said. "Literally. We have true-to-life color portraits of it from every angle, and it bears an incriminating inscription etched into the silver. How many hairpins matching that description do you think we're likely to find in Rotherham's rooms?"

"One," Gracie said. "I hope."

"It's stolen property," Philippa tried again. "What if some maid or passer-by sees one of you and claims your family was in possession of a stolen object? You'll be able to immediately hand it back to its rightful owner."

"Rightful owner's *sister*," said Gracie. "Technically."

"Rightful original thief," Elizabeth corrected. "I

believe the actual owner has yet to be told her hairpin is missing?"

Gracie's face turned pink.

"May Theodosia never learn of it," she muttered.

"Our proximity is also convenient in the event a distraction is needed," Philippa said.

"Or extra guards," Gracie added. "I can stun a miscreant with my reticule. I filled it with rocks."

Philippa and Elizabeth stared at her.

Gracie lifted her chin. "I don't trust rakes anymore."

"Very well," Elizabeth said. "Not because of your portable rock collection, but because possession of stolen property can be difficult to explain away in certain circumstances. Stay here, *do nothing*, and the moment we've retrieved the hairpin, we shall place it in your hands."

"Thank you." Gracie's shoulders visibly relaxed.

Philippa caught sight of movement across the street. "Oh *no*."

Not one, but three different interlopers were approaching number 86 from three different directions. A bewigged and liveried footman from the left, a handsome young gentleman from the right, and a farmhand pulling a cart full of milk bottles from the center of the street.

"What's happening?" Gracie whispered.

"Deliveries... afternoon calls..." Philippa clenched her fists in frustration. "There are too many witnesses. We'll have to call the whole thing off."

"Pah," said Elizabeth without turning around. "Those are all Wynchesters."

Philippa stared at her. "What? They are? How?"

Elizabeth removed a dainty handkerchief from her bodice and used the pink embroidered corner to buff a smudge from the head of her iron serpent. "I presume they've breached the residence?"

Philippa lifted her gaze back to number 86. All of the Wynchester brothers had vanished. The "milkman" had apparently gone round to the servants' entrance.

"Yes," she managed. "They're inside."

"What about that one?" Gracie pointed. "Did another of your brothers disguise himself as Lord Bussington?"

"Of course not." Philippa pushed Gracie's hand back down to her side. "That's the real Lord Bussington, coincidentally also out for a stroll on his afternoon constitutional." She jerked her eyes over to Elizabeth. "Er... right?"

"Yes," said Elizabeth. "Stay here whilst I bludgeon him."

"*No*," Gracie gasped. "Think of the attention you'd draw."

"We needn't do anything," Philippa told them both. "He'll walk right past us."

He did not walk right past them.

"Why, Miss York," he said, as though the other two women flanking Philippa were invisible. "Just the young lady I was hoping to see."

"You weren't hoping that," said Philippa. "There would be no reason to assume I'd be loitering on a random street corner at this precise moment."

"What I mean is," Bussington said smoothly, "I was hoping to secure a set or two as your dance partner at the next ball."

"Which ball?"

"Any ball." Lord Bussington gestured expansively.

Philippa narrowed her eyes. "Did my mother increase my dowry again?"

This time, Gracie kicked her in the leg.

Bussington coughed into his gloved hand. "I should hope you know a true gentleman believes marriage is more than a monetary transaction."

"I doubt it," Philippa said. "That's why my mother keeps raising my dowry."

"Miss York is tremendously flattered," Gracie interrupted, batting her eyelashes ferociously as though attempting to imbue Philippa with a flirtatious nature using transference. "Of course she would love to dance with you on some other occasion when she is not so dreadfully busy."

"Busy... loitering on a street corner?" Lord Bussington said doubtfully.

"I don't like to dance," said Philippa. "And I don't want a husband."

Particularly one who met her parents' requirement of "excessive pride" and a "firm hand." She did not care to know if Bussington fit those conditions.

"Extremely busy," Gracie repeated. "We're out of

sorts because you've caught us at an awkward time. We must say goodbye now, but please feel free to beg a dance again when you see her at that ball."

Bussington frowned. "Which ball?"

"*Any* ball." Gracie waved him off. "*Au revoir*, fair Bussington. Go home and buff your dancing slippers!"

He backed away as though regretting having stopped at all. At five paces, he turned to hurry down the street toward Grosvenor Square, pausing only twice to send befuddled glances over his shoulder. At last, he was too far away to be seen in the distance.

"He was *trying* to flirt with you," said Gracie.

Philippa lifted a shoulder. "I wasn't trying to flirt with *him*."

"Clearly," said Gracie. "God save us, if that was your best effort."

"You two should have let me give him a little tap with my sword stick," said Elizabeth. "It would have been less painful."

"I'm not good at flirting," Philippa said.

"Shock," said Elizabeth. "This is my expression of abject shock."

"I can teach you," Gracie suggested.

"You shan't be flirting anymore either," Philippa reminded her. "Isn't that why you're carrying a reticule filled with rocks?"

"I won't flirt with *rakes*," Gracie clarified. "There'll be no more private escapades in a darkened garden. But one needn't be alone to have a proper flirt with someone. Banter is the best part of every assembly. You should try it."

Philippa wrinkled her nose. "What if he tries to kiss me?"

"Not everyone who flirts with you intends to kiss you," Gracie said in exasperation. "Even Rotherham..."

Philippa's and Elizabeth's faces swiveled in Gracie's direction.

Her cheeks went bright red.

"Even Rotherham what?" prompted Elizabeth.

"Rotherham the inveterate rake who swings any miss in a skirt into the closest closet for a tup," Philippa added helpfully.

"Oh, very well," said Gracie. "If you must know, he didn't kiss me."

"Didn't kiss you?" Elizabeth repeated carefully.

Gracie sighed. "Didn't kiss me, didn't paw at me, didn't fill my ears with love words and lies. He talked about the weather for a mind-deadening length of time, then touched my cheek and said I was a sweet girl and that we should head back inside. What kind of rake fails to act rakishly when he has the opportunity?"

"My favorite kind," Philippa replied. "I wouldn't have wanted him to kiss me. His lips have locked with every other lady in London. He's the Blarney Stone of men."

"Kissed every other mouth except mine," Gracie said. "With me, there was a distinct lack of kissing."

"Mayhap he was waiting for you to begin," Elizabeth suggested.

Gracie's face flushed even darker. "I... may have..."

"You tried to rake him?" Philippa said in surprise.

"Not *rake* him, exactly." Gracie didn't meet their eyes. "I thought I'd give him a peck on the cheek to see if there were any sparks before we headed back inside."

"What happened?" asked Elizabeth.

"He flinched out of reach as though I were a maggot," Gracie mumbled.

Philippa stared at her. "If Rotherham the Rake didn't lure you to the rear garden to ravish you..."

"Then stealing your hairpin was always the plan," Elizabeth finished. "But why?"

Gracie frowned. "It's a nice hairpin?"

"True," Elizabeth said. "I've seen the pictures."

"But anything could have gone wrong," Philippa said. "You might have caught him stealing the hairpin. Or someone else might have caught you both alone in the garden. If he didn't want to kiss you, being compromised and forced to wed wouldn't help matters."

"We're missing something," Elizabeth mused, drumming her fingers on her coiled iron serpent. "What are we missing?"

"The hairpin," panted a voice just behind them. "And Lord Rotherham."

THE RAKE MISTAKE

They swung about to see Chloe jogging up from around the corner.

"What do you mean?" asked Gracie. "What happened?"

"Nothing happened." Chloe came to a stop right in front of them and lay a hand on her stomach as she caught her breath. "I ate five different ices waiting for him to arrive, and he never did."

"Mayhap he skipped ices today," said Elizabeth, "and went straight to Hyde Park."

Chloe shook her head. "I tried that next. He wasn't anywhere. I asked around, and no one has seen him."

Gracie's eyes widened. "He's not still in his *rooms*, is he?"

They all turned to look, just as the liveried footman exited number 86 and closed the door tight behind him.

The slender, brown-haired gentleman was already halfway down the street. He tipped his hat in the ladies' direction before disappearing around the corner.

The footman vanished in the opposite direction, writing in a small book. It was Graham in livery and a white wig.

Rusty wheels squeaked as the milk cart made a renewed appearance. The farmhand left a few bottles on a front step, then pulled the cart across the road toward the ladies. It was Jacob Wynchester in disguise.

"I had no chance to search Rotherham," Chloe told Jacob. "He never showed."

"I'm not surprised." Only the bottom half of Jacob's face was visible beneath the broken brim of his hat. "Their lodgings are empty. He's gone."

"*Gone?*" Gracie blurted out. "He can't be *gone*."

"He and his brother both," Jacob confirmed. "Those rooms were rented. There were no personal items left behind. Everything they had, they took with them."

"To Kent." Philippa groaned. "Their father's country estate."

CHAPTER 6

Philippa managed to hurry Gracie, Elizabeth, and Chloe down the street, through her front door, and into Philippa's bluestocking parlor without running into her mother.

The reprieve would not last for long.

She would have preferred to accept the Wynchesters' offer to reassemble at their house, but Mrs. York expected her daughter home from her walk within the hour, and Gracie's family believed her to be in Philippa's parlor, not miles away. Inciting a panicked manhunt would not aid their ever-increasing need for stealth—and swiftness.

"Tell us about the Kent estate," said Chloe. "You know these people personally. Have you been inside the Strathmore country home?"

"I haven't," Gracie answered.

"I have," Philippa said, feeling a sliver of hope.

"Have you got an invitation for later this summer?"

Philippa's shoulders curved. "No."

"An invitation for August wouldn't help, anyway." Gracie's face was pale. "We need to recover the hairpin *now*, before the banns are read. If Theodosia loses the love of her life, she'll never forgive me. And if he jilts her publicly..."

"She'll be ruined," Chloe finished. "What we need is—"

The parlor door flung open, causing the handkerchief in the keyhole to flutter to the floor.

"I brought tea for you and Gracie," Philippa's mother sang out, followed by a barely concealed shriek of horror at finding two other guests in the parlor.

"This is my mother, Mrs. York. Mother, you know the Duchess of Faircliffe, of course. And this other young lady is... my friend Elizabeth."

A highly improper introduction, for which Philippa would be roundly rebuked later, but it was perhaps best not to divulge Elizabeth's identity as a Wynchester.

"This will not do," Mother said, wringing her hands. "It won't do at all."

A kitchen maid hung back uncertainly behind her mistress, bearing a small silver tray with service for three... indicating Mother had intended not just to bring tea, but to invite herself to it as well.

"How kind of you," Chloe said, rising to her feet

to accept the tray. "And how prescient. Poor Elizabeth breaks out in spots if she drinks tea, which makes this service for three exactly perfect. Thank you so much for your hospitality. We shan't trouble you any further."

Very neatly done.

Mother's startled eyes bounced from one face to the other. She could not now contradict this interpretation of events, or protest that the third teacup was meant for her, and not for the Duchess of Faircliffe.

"Very well," Mother said, shooting Philippa a look that warned A Talk would occur later. "I'll leave you to your tea."

She paused meaningfully, giving Philippa plenty of time to send the maid for another cup and saucer.

"Thank you, Mother," Philippa said instead. "You are an exemplary hostess, and all that is kind and thoughtful."

Mother looked as though she was grinding her teeth into powder, but at last spun on her heel and stalked from the room, nudging the door open even wider as she sailed out into the corridor.

"How is your Greek?" Gracie whispered to Elizabeth.

Elizabeth's eyes widened. "I enjoy baklava?"

"Baklava might be Turkish," Philippa whispered back.

"*Parlons en français*," Chloe said, switching to French. "It's our secret language."

"I see," said Elizabeth, in a tone that implied she did not see at all, but was willing to play along. "*C'est un secret intéressant.*"

Unsurprisingly, her accent was phenomenal. Elizabeth could likely mimic Napoleon Bonaparte himself.

"How long will Lord Rotherham remain at his parents' home in Kent?" Chloe asked.

"For at least a fortnight." Philippa poured the tea. "Lord and Lady Strathmore always throw a 'welcome home' gala shortly after they and their sons retire to the country for the summer."

"Perfect." Elizabeth lifted her teacup. "We strike then."

"We aren't invited," Gracie reminded her.

"Pah." Elizabeth rolled her eyes. "Who needs invitations? We have an entire *library* of ruses."

"Mark it down as my next reading circle recommendation," Gracie murmured.

Chloe and Elizabeth began to argue in rapid-fire French.

"First, there's reconnaissance." Elizabeth drummed her fingers on her cane. "Shall we do 'Monks and Marbles'?"

"Not enough time," said Chloe. "Think spatial, not schedules. Perhaps 'Hell in a Handbasket'?"

Elizabeth shook her head. "Too far to take the trained owls."

"What about interior maps? We'll need those."

"Mm. Then either 'Bob the Kangaroo' or 'Dueling

Dominos.'

Chloe wrinkled her nose. "Both of those require a close vantage point."

"Then what is your suggestion?" Elizabeth demanded. "'Tippets and Teapots?'"

"I can help," Philippa said.

Chloe shook her head. "Better to let the experts manage it."

"You've never even been there," Philippa pointed out. "It will be easier if I'm involved—"

"No, it won't," Elizabeth murmured.

"—as well as the rest of the reading circle—"

"Definitely not," Chloe agreed.

"—and I can arrange as close a vantage point as we need," Philippa finished. "Lady Quarrington lives nearby, and she would love to unexpectedly open her home to me and ten or twenty of my dearest friends."

"Would she?" Elizabeth said doubtfully.

"I thought you swore off all social contact with your cousin," Gracie said.

"That's why she'd be thrilled to host me," Philippa replied. "Especially if I come crawling. It will be as though she won."

"How 'near' is 'nearby?'" asked Chloe.

"Neighbors," Philippa answered. "Only a hedgerow divides their properties. Although, stately country homes being what they are, that still puts a considerable distance between the houses."

"It works," Elizabeth admitted.

"It's splendid." Chloe grinned at Philippa. "We accept."

"I can't invite your brothers," Philippa said quickly. "My cousin will expect an all-female group of bluestockings."

"Never mind them," said Elizabeth. "They always find a way."

"There you rascals are," a quavery voice scolded from the doorway. "Have you seen my spectacles?"

They turned to see Great-Aunt Wynchester doddering through the open doorway.

"Your spectacles are in your hair, Aunt," said Chloe.

"They are?" Great-Aunt Wynchester patted her voluminous white hair in surprise. "So they are!"

Philippa's mother burst into the room right behind her.

"This will not do." Mother wrung her hands as she glared from guest to guest. "This will not do at all. Once a week is bad enough—"

"Is 'occasional' hospitality a lesser crime?" Philippa asked.

"Thursday was *yesterday*," Mother snapped. "You can't have friends again until next week! In fact—no new books until you're betrothed. I won't hear a single word of argument. You will be the death of me, Philippa!"

"Of course you deserve a respite," Philippa said soothingly. "You'll be pleased to know that I'll be out from underfoot for the next fortnight."

"What?" Mother screeched. "Where do you think you're going?"

"To visit Lady Quarrington," Philippa replied calmly.

Her mother gaped at her like a fish out of water, then visibly calmed.

"That is a good idea," Mother said with rare approval. "The marchioness is a fine influence. She may even be able to find you a suitor. Doesn't she live next door to the Strathmore estate? Both sons are still unwed. They may be in residence."

"Might they? What a coincidence," Philippa murmured.

"Take a chaperone," Mother commanded. "Not your usual attendant—Octavia dresses you well, but she is far too young and lets you get away with too much poppycock."

"Er," said Philippa. "I'll take... Great-Aunt Wynchester."

Mother and Great-Aunt Wynchester both made twin strangled noises in their throats.

"Very well," said Philippa. "I'll take Great-Aunt Wynchester *and* Octavia. Between the two of them, they'll never let me out of their sight. In fact, I'll be taking the entire reading circle with me."

"Oh?" Mother gave a pointed look at the tea tray she hadn't been invited to share, then back to Philippa. "In that case, I shall join you."

"It isn't necessary for you to take such a journey. In fact, perhaps this will be the moment Lady Quarrington and I put our quarrel behind us. My cousin and I—"

"—shan't resolve a single thing without me there to guide you," Mother said firmly.

"I thought you had plans with your friends? You find mine so vexing. Wouldn't it be more relaxing to—"

"If I don't go," Mother said, "I suppose I shall spend my time organizing the parlor. So many dusty books clogging our perfectly nice shelves. I am certain I can put things to rights."

Philippa's teeth shut with a click. This was not an empty threat. The last time she had defied her parents, some of Philippa's most treasured rare illuminated manuscripts were sold off, and the contact information of the buyer "accidentally" lost.

"Very well." She forced a smile. "Shall we pack our trunks?"

CHAPTER 7

"A free-standing turret for no reason." Elizabeth turned in a slow circle, spyglass in hand. "We must have Baron Vanderbean erect one at home posthaste."

Philippa, the Wynchester women, and half of the reading circle gathered in Lady Quarrington's elegant belvedere fifty feet behind her house.

The two-story tall, open structure offered stunning panoramas from all angles, but most pairs of eyes were trained on the half-acre Strathmore property next door. Great-Aunt Wynchester handed Philippa a spyglass.

Instead of a belvedere, the Strathmore garden boasted an open rotunda, large enough for musicians to perform whilst protected from inclement weather by the curved dome overhead. Wrought-iron garden chairs were to be set up surrounding the rotunda, so that all guests would have an equally fine view of the performance.

There were no such chairs visible at the moment. Just the gorgeous garden, with its famed row of bright hibiscus and lilac bushes that attracted hundreds of colorful butterflies in certain months, and a lovely pergola with sweet-smelling honeysuckle covering the latticed roof and tumbling artfully down.

Gracie was not here to enjoy the view. She was indoors with an unfeigned megrim. This morning's scandal columns had once again mentioned the hairpin belonging to Lord Rotherham's mystery lover. Gracie was being careful to keep out of sight lest Rotherham spot her and suspect mischief afoot.

"When you said a hedgerow divided the two properties," said Elizabeth, "I expected something... much taller than myself. This hedge is short enough for a trained horse to jump."

"Our horses are trained to pull carriages," Philippa said. "They can't even jump over holes in the road."

"Graham could jump it," Elizabeth said. "He could do it *standing* on a horse."

"Subtlety," Chloe reminded her. "This case calls for discretion, not theatrics."

"A waste of a good hedgerow," Elizabeth muttered.

Their two brothers had accompanied them, dressed in white wigs and the black-and-gold

Wynchester livery. Amongst the ton, it was fashionable for footmen to be a "matched pair"—similar height and build. The brothers could not look less alike.

Graham was taller, his natural ringlets floppier, his athletic body leaner, and his skin a golden bronze compared to his brother's rich brown. Jacob's shoulders were wider, his muscles more defined, his black curls freshly cropped, and his livery covered in… cat fur? Mongoose? Leopard? One never knew with Jacob.

As the Wynchester sisters' "footmen," the brothers were free to come and go without question. They were working on befriending the servants next door, as well as interviewing other townsfolk. Little passed without a servant learning about it. Which was how Graham had discovered the information about Gracie's lost pin had arrived to the hands of the scandal columnist courtesy of a footman employed at Rotherham's Brook Street lodgings.

Not that they needed more circumstantial evidence against him. What they needed was to find the stolen jewelry.

Philippa turned to Great-Aunt Wynchester. "I'm sorry I claimed you instead of my lady's maid yesterday, with no warning. You had no idea what we were talking about, so of course you were taken aback. I wasn't going to make you dress me."

Great-Aunt Wynchester stared at her, wide-eyed.

"I was just thinking it would be easier to plot

stratagems *without* Octavia hanging on every word," Philippa continued. "Luckily, I've assigned Octavia to Gracie in the meantime, so we can scheme freely."

"I'm going to have a stroll," Great-Aunt Wynchester barked, then tottered away before anyone could stop her. She crossed the Quarrington garden toward the main road, forty yards from the belvedere.

"Is she heading toward... the Strathmore residence?" Florentia gasped.

"What in heaven's name does she intend to do there?" asked Lady Eunice.

"God only knows," murmured Chloe. "My brother Graham's expertise is London, but he's begun a new album for Kent. He adores any opportunity to add new intelligence to his collection." She pulled a leather-bound journal from her wicker basket. "I have his notes on the Lords Strathmore and family."

Damaris frowned. "Isn't there only one Lord Strathmore?"

"At a time, yes," Elizabeth agreed. "Graham's research spans several generations."

"What good can it do us to know... whatever he knows about Rotherham's great-great-grandfather?" Florentia enquired.

"That's the thing," said Chloe. "You never know what you need to know until you need to know it. That's why it's always best to know as much as one can in advance."

"From a certain perspective, that's how our

reading circle began," Philippa said. "We didn't start reading novels until recently. We were piqued that *men* have clubs and societies for every sort of scholarly topic, yet ladies' brains are deemed too fragile to allow in."

"So we made our own," Damaris said. "Like the Royal Society, but better, because *we're* in it."

"Ooh," said Sybil. "Can we be the Unroyal Society of Ladies Whose Brains are Better than Men's?"

"No," said Philippa. "Absolutely not."

"I like it," Florentia said. "But it won't fit on a medallion. We need something shorter."

"No brooches," said Philippa.

She could not abide the heartache if her parents dismantled the group only for a brooch to arrive in the post, proclaiming her membership in a sisterhood that no longer existed.

Elizabeth's eyes narrowed beyond the hedgerow. "Theodosia's hairpin is somewhere in that house."

Chloe nodded. "We presume. Graham has investigated all known fences, jewelers, and pawnbrokers, and found nothing. His contacts will continue to monitor the situation for news."

"Rotherham has plenty of coin. Whatever his reasons for taking the hairpin, it wasn't because he was starving in the streets. He may never intend to part with the pin."

"I know from experience it can take far longer than you think to search for something that's well hidden." Chloe gripped the belvedere's balustrade and grimaced. "Tommy and I once searched a simple town house for more than a month. This is ten times that size."

Elizabeth leaned on her cane. "How long until the 'welcome home' gala?"

"One week," Philippa replied.

"One week," Sybil repeated. "To do what couldn't be accomplished in a month. It's impossible."

"Pah," said Elizabeth. "Wynchesters achieve the impossible three times a day."

"Ladies!" trilled a merry voice from Lady Quarrington's rear door. "I've brought tea!"

"Does your mother ever stop bringing tea?" Chloe murmured.

Philippa shook her head. "Only under duress."

"It's not even her house," Florentia said, impressed.

"All houses are Mother's house," Philippa said. "Mayhap we should send *her* in to find the hairpin."

Elizabeth brightened. "Would she?"

"She would not." Philippa's stomach soured at the thought. "She would inform Gracie's family of her 'unfortunate indiscretion' and make the situation a hundred times worse."

Just as Mother and a small army of maids bearing tea trays reached the belvedere, a large dog burst through the hedgerow and came bounding up behind her.

Mother shrieked and threw her hands into the air,

causing several of the maids to do the same before they even ascertained the source of danger.

Cakes and sandwiches went flying.

The maids bearing trays of teapots managed to keep hold of their trays and their senses, and made identical expressions of *aww* to discover the disruption was nothing more than a friendly, ancient Alpine Mastiff…. who was deeply enjoying a sudden bounty of cakes and sandwiches.

"Get that mongrel out of my sight at once!" Mother demanded.

"It's *my* dog," Chloe called out. "And it's a Mastiff."

"*Is* it our dog?" Elizabeth whispered.

"I recognize the snuffbox strapped to his collar," Chloe whispered back.

"I politely request Your Grace to get your beast under control!" Mother shrilled.

The beast in question was lying on his back in the grass, tongue lolling from his mouth in abject joy as one of the maids gave his furry belly a quick rub. The fur about his muzzle had gone white with age.

And there was indeed a snuffbox attached to his collar.

In all of the paintings and illustrations Philippa could recall, Alpine Mastiffs bore a sturdy wooden barrel attached to their collars, containing restorative fluids for snowbound travelers in need. Not a snuffbox.

Then again, the Wynchesters had never been ordinary before. Why would they begin now?

"Does your dog take snuff?" Philippa asked politely.

"It's not for him," Chloe said. "It's for me."

"*You* take snuff?" gasped Florentia.

She and the other ladies hurried down from the belvedere to the grass to meet the new arrival.

"Don't worry about tea, Mother," Philippa said. "We'll return inside when we're peckish."

Mother harrumphed and stalked back into the safety of Lady Quarrington's home.

Philippa would *definitely* receive a proper earful about this later.

"Don't you worry about the tea, either," Philippa said to her cousin's maids. "Lay whatever is salvageable, and return to your posts with our apologies and deepest gratitude."

The maids curtsied and entered the belvedere to arrange what they could of the tea.

Chloe knelt next to the Mastiff and popped open his snuffbox. A folded note tumbled into her palm.

Walk with me.
Zeus

"Well, that's simple enough." Chloe rubbed behind the Mastiff's ears. "How do you do this fine afternoon, Zeus? Shall we have a little walk to pass the time?"

"How can we walk him anywhere?" asked Philippa. "He's carrying a snuffbox, not a leash."

"I keep a length of rope in my basket," Chloe replied.

"Of course you do," Philippa murmured. In case one needed to descend a steep cliff or the Tower of London.

At this point, if Chloe pulled a rhinoceros from her basket, Philippa oughtn't even to blink.

"Enjoy the tea," Elizabeth told the reading circle. "Chloe and I shall take this old boy for a meander."

"And I as well," Philippa said quickly. "Before my mother returns to stop me."

Chloe tied her rope to Zeus's collar and straightened.

Zeus remained on his back in anticipation of more belly rubs.

"Come on, Zeus," Elizabeth coaxed. "Shall we hunt for squirrels?"

After much cajoling, Zeus lumbered back to his feet and ambled gamely around the house and down the drive to the road.

Rather than turn toward the Strathmore property as Philippa expected, Zeus and Chloe turned in the opposite direction.

"We're not going to casually stroll past Lord Rotherham's residence?" Philippa enquired.

"Zeus is leading," Elizabeth answered. "If we were

meant to go another way, there would have been a signal."

"Like what?" Philippa asked.

Chloe shrugged. "You know it when you see it."

Philippa was not at all certain she would correctly interpret any signals coming from the Wynchesters.

As soon as they rounded a low brick wall, putting them out of sight from both stately homes, including the Quarrington belvedere, two figures in white wigs and black-and-gold livery emerged from a hedgerow.

"Attack," said Chloe.

Zeus flopped to the ground belly-up, as if awaiting stomach rubs.

"*Attaque, s'il te plaît,*" Chloe tried again.

Zeus sneezed and flopped onto his belly, giving his tail a single flick before closing his eyes.

Chloe arched her brow at her brothers. "Is Rotherham supposed to be frightened of this ancient dog?"

"Kent was too far to travel with a python or a Highland tiger," Jacob explained.

"Or a python *and* a Highland tiger, which was Jacob's first plan," Graham added.

"It was a good plan," Jacob muttered.

Philippa blinked. "With a what?"

Jacob knelt beside Zeus and fed him a scrap of dried meat from his pocket. "Have you heard from—? Oh, here she is."

Philippa turned to see Great-Aunt Wynchester hobbling up the road.

"Maps." Great-Aunt Wynchester handed a sheaf of papers to Chloe.

Graham did the same. "Schedules."

"Excellent work," Chloe said as she studied each page.

"Er," said Philippa. "Maps of what?"

"Exterior maps of the house and grounds," Chloe replied. "Height, width, and location of doors and windows, distance from other object and landmarks. The usual."

"And the schedules?"

"Staff schedules," Graham explained. "The times of day different servants take and leave their posts, where they're expected to be and what they're expected to do, and when. That sort of thing."

"Oh," Philippa said faintly. "Of course."

"Any surprises?" Elizabeth asked.

"One." Graham's brown eyes sparkled. "Despite rejecting Lord Rotherham's suit, Miss Ipsley is a dear friend of the family. Not only was she invited to the gala, Miss Ipsley has already accepted her invitation."

Chloe whistled. "Awkward."

"Rumor has it, if he begs her hand again, she'll cut him no matter who is present."

"He deserves as much," said Philippa. "A man in love should not be scurrying about stealing kisses and hairpins and trysting with other women."

Graham inclined his head. "By all accounts, Miss Ipsley shares those feelings precisely."

"What now?" asked Elizabeth. "We spend the next week refining our reconnaissance?"

Great-Aunt Wynchester pulled her spectacles from her wiry hair. "We need to get inside. We have to map the interior of the house. The paths to, and the escape routes from, Lord Rotherham's private chambers and anywhere else he's likely to frequent. Visibility, squeaky floors..."

"There's a small garden party in two days," Graham said. "Tea, violins, that sort of thing. Philippa, can you obtain an invitation?"

"I can arrange one for myself," she said. "Being Lady Quarrington's cousin and guest ought to do the trick. But I won't be able to beg invitations for twenty other people."

"Mayhap just two more?" Elizabeth winked at Chloe. "The Duchess of Faircliffe and her dear aunt?"

Philippa nodded. "I'll do my best."

CHAPTER 8

"But—But—" Mother flapped her hands in dismay at the sight of Philippa's reading circle tying bonnets on their heads at the front door. "I thought we might all sit down with poor Miss Kimball for a cup of tea!"

Gracie would rather the reading circle make progress on her problem.

With less than twenty-four hours remaining before tomorrow's garden party reconnaissance mission, this might be one of the ladies' final opportunities to discuss stratagems with the Wynchester brothers.

Philippa touched her mother's elbow. "I'll have tea with you when we return from our walk, if you like."

Mother jerked her arm away.

"I can have tea with *you* whenever I please," she hissed. "Try to think of your poor mother once in a while. You're always monopolizing Lady Eunice's time."

Ah. So it was not fellowship that she sought, but proximity to higher rank.

Mother's eternal quest, and the reason for her continued disappointment in Philippa.

"Being your daughter isn't important enough?" she said dryly.

"You'll be important once you've married a title," Mother snapped. "See that you spend time with Lord Rotherham tomorrow. He is in want of a bride."

"I solemnly swear I intend to have words with him," Philippa assured her.

Whilst her mother harrumphed, Philippa slipped out of the door to join her friends.

Chloe was near the front of the pack, leading Zeus out to the main road.

"This is so diverting!" Lady Eunice said in French, clapping her hands together. "I've never taken part in a covert mission before."

"We're not the least bit covert," Philippa pointed out. "We're a dozen bonneted ladies and an ancient Mastiff."

"That's it," said Sybil, eyes shining. "We're the Covert Club."

"Or," said Damaris, "the Covert *Caper* Club."

"Absolutely not," said Philippa. "And be quiet. Someone could hear you."

"We're speaking our secret language," Sybil said.

"French is only incomprehensible to my mother,"

Philippa reminded her. "Entire countries speak French."

"Next week is Greek week!" Florentia gave a little bounce. "I daresay *ancient* Greek is properly covert."

"How about the Hairpin Rescue Society?" said Sybil.

"What?" Damaris goggled at her. "Are we only to be rescuing hairpins from now on?"

"The hairpin is incidental to our activities." Lady Eunice's eyes sparkled with mischief. "The important part is the heist."

"That's it!" Florentia's face lit up. "*Heist Club.*"

The other ladies raised their fists in delight. "Heist Club!"

"For the last time," Philippa said. "You cannot name a club after the secret clandestine activity you don't want people to know that the club is furtively doing."

"We fight on behalf of others," said Lady Eunice. "We're a Fight Club."

Florentia wrinkled her nose. "'Heist Club' is far superior."

"I'll commission brooches," said Damaris.

"I'll create scented soaps," said Sybil.

"We're not having a charity sale to raise money for a ladies' reading circle that is definitely not called Heist Club," Philippa said.

"Literature is only one of our interests," Lady Eunice countered. "We are cosmopolitan women of many and sundry talents."

"And we're here," said Chloe.

Her brothers Graham and Jacob emerged from hedgerows on opposite sides of the road. In Graham's hand was a journal. In Jacob's arms was his mongoose.

Zeus barked in delight. The mongoose made a high-pitched trill that almost sounded like the call of a bird.

"Shh, Orville." Jacob stroked the mongoose's fur.

Zeus barked louder.

Orville let out a shrill hissing scream. Jacob placed it around his neck like a living fur cravat. The mongoose yawned and licked its pink nose. Or else it was sticking its tongue out at poor Zeus.

"Why did you bring the mongoose again?" Graham murmured.

"You never know when you might need a mongoose," Jacob whispered back. He turned to Chloe. "Did you bring everything?"

She handed him her basket.

Jacob knelt before the dog. Zeus sniffed at the mongoose draped about Jacob's neck. Orville responded by swatting at the dog's nose, causing him to sit back on his haunches in surprise.

Jacob fitted Zeus with a sturdy leather harness. "Use your training."

"What is your ancient dog trained for?" Florentia enquired.

Jacob scratched behind Zeus's ears. "Espionage."

"Oh." Lady Eunice exchanged a glance with Philippa. "That seems useful."

Jacob pulled a charming wooden barrel about the size of an ale mug from the basket and set it on the grass.

Damaris sent a doubtful look at the warm June sun overhead. "Are we in danger of being trapped in an avalanche of snow?"

"I hope not," said Jacob. "We didn't plan for that."

He affixed Zeus's snuffbox to his collar with leather straps.

Chloe picked up the wooden barrel and attempted to open it, with no result. Graham held out a hand, and she tossed him the barrel. He spent several long moments in concentration before shrugging and throwing the barrel back to Chloe.

"I suppose," said Philippa, "it is meant to carry liquid?"

"It can carry anything that fits inside. Except liquid. I poked holes in it." Jacob opened Zeus's snuffbox and pulled out a piece of carrot, which he fed to the Mastiff, before rising to his feet. "Here is the call to make when you want Zeus to come quickly."

He formed his lips into an O and made a sound indistinguishable to Philippa from the melody of a robin.

"Mightn't it be easier just to say... 'Here, Zeus?'" Florentia enquired.

"It's subterfuge," said Damaris.

"The Subterfuge Sisterhood!" whispered Lady Eunice.

"Stop it," Philippa whispered back.

Damaris practiced the whistle. Zeus turned about at once and bounded over to her.

"What if there are actual robins in the garden?" Florentia asked. "Will Zeus come to us or go to the birds?"

"And why do we *want* Zeus to come to us?" Lady Eunice added. "What does he do, besides eat carrots and expect belly rubs?"

"Those are very good traits," cooed Damaris, currently in the act of belly-rubbing. "Who has the softest belly? Is it you? Does Zeus have the softest belly?"

"He'll definitely come if you call him," Jacob assured Florentia. "He's trained to distinguish proper birdsong from inferior human renditions. And as to his skills—"

The sound of distant laughter carried on the breeze. Jacob and Graham took a subservient step back just as two well-dressed gentlemen strode into view, chatting and smiling.

The dastardly Lord Rotherham and his brother, Mr. Briggs.

"My heavens." A grin bloomed on Rotherham's face. "What a pleasure to cross paths with so many beautiful ladies."

"I'll show you what would give *me* pleasure,"

Damaris muttered behind Philippa. "I'll attack you with a mongoose."

Rotherham's eyes turned in Philippa's direction. "Did you say something?"

"Not to you," she said flatly.

The rake stepped closer.

His brother, Mr. Briggs, hovered just to one side as though ready to leap to his brother's aid at any moment. "Oh. The 'bluestockings.' I don't know why you ladies bother reading things you cannot understand."

Philippa wondered if he'd understand a parasol to the head.

"Miss York," rakish Lord Rotherham said warmly. "We've not seen each other in weeks."

Philippa stared back at him without responding.

"Dare I hope you'll be attending my parents' gala next week?" Rotherham enquired.

"*Our* parents," Briggs corrected.

"If you haven't got an invitation..." Rotherham lifted Philippa's hand. "I'll have my mother rectify that error posthaste."

"*Our* mother," Briggs muttered.

Philippa returned her hand to her side before Rotherham could kiss it. "I have an invitation."

"Splendid." He tipped his hat. "I'll save a dance for you then."

There was nothing Philippa wished for less.

Fortunately, Rotherham did not seem to require verbal acceptance of this pronouncement. He and his brother continued up the road as though the interaction had gone precisely as planned.

"Miss Ipsley will be at that party," Graham whispered. "What is his game?"

The sound of approaching horse hoofs thundered up the connecting road and a mail coach pulled into view.

"Whoa!" cried a female passenger from atop the overloaded carriage.

The horses slowed, and the passenger leapt to the ground.

"*Theodosia?*" Philippa blurted out in surprise.

"Philippa!" Theodosia threw herself into Philippa's arms. "You must save me. My life is over."

Graham tossed a coin to the driver and was currently removing Theodosia's valise from the mail coach.

Theodosia pulled a crumpled scrap of paper from her reticule and shoved it into Philippa's hands. "*This* was in the morning paper. I know this is Gracie's doing, and I mean to have her undo it at once."

Philippa unfolded the paper and read aloud. "'Do we have a name for rakish Lord R—'s latest conquest? It seems the lady's token has frequently adorned the tresses of a Miss T— K—. One wonders if Mr. V— is aware of their tryst...'"

"Miss T— K— is *me*." Theodosia's eyes were wide with panic. "Mr. V— is my betrothed. Or at least, he is for now. He asked me about the gossip when he came to visit me this morning. I said it was either a lie or a misunderstanding, because my hairpin is right upstairs in my jewelry box. I went to retrieve it to prove my innocence, and *it was gone,* just like my sister!"

"Oh dear," Philippa said. "What did Mr. Voss say when you told him you were not in possession of the hairpin after all?"

"I didn't tell him," Theodosia answered. "I sneaked out of the window and took the first coach to Sevenoaks. There's nothing I can say that will prove my innocence. *Gracie* has to remedy this. The first banns are tomorrow!"

Philippa fought the urge to cover her face with her hand. "But what will Mr. Voss think now that you've run away in the middle of a conversation?"

"I left him a note," Theodosia said. "I promised things aren't as dire as they appear, and that my heart is true. I asked him to give me two days and I would explain everything. *Please* tell me things aren't as dire as they appear!"

"They're quite dire," said Damaris. "Rotherham definitely has your hairpin and the gossips know it."

"*Augh!*" Theodosia crashed forward into Philippa's arms.

"But we're getting it back," Philippa assured her.

"A week from today, at the Strathmore gala," Lady Eunice added.

"But I *haven't* a week." Theodosia lifted her tear-stained face from Philippa's shoulder. "If I don't have that hairpin in my possession by Monday, I won't have a husband, either."

Philippa exchanged a glance with Chloe. "Garden party?"

Chloe nodded. "Garden party."

"But tomorrow's gathering is an intimate affair," protested Florentia. "Philippa is the only one of us with an invitation!"

"First rule of Wynchester," said Chloe. "Do it anyway."

CHAPTER 9

*P*hilippa's reading circle and the other Wynchester ladies huddled in the belvedere with a view over the hedgerow into the Strathmore estate. All of the windows and doors were open to air out the house. The afternoon was brisk and only partly cloudy—perfect for a garden party.

They watched as liveried footmen placed a ring of chairs around the open rotunda, into which climbed a trio of debutantes, each bearing a violin case.

The party was ready to begin.

"There aren't enough chairs," said Sybil.

"Of course there aren't enough chairs," Damaris replied. "We're not invited, remember? We shall simply storm through the hedgerow—"

"No one will storm through any hedgerows," Philippa said. "You will walk next door to the proper entrance, with me. There are more chairs."

"And Gracie?" Florentia asked.

"Gracie and her sister will arrive first, with Lady Quarrington and Mrs. York," Chloe confirmed. "Not only will this establish the precedent of invited guests bringing a guest of their own, Lord Rotherham will be particularly invested in not causing a scene with Gracie."

Lady Eunice lifted her violin case. "True. That inglorious hater-of-books Miss Ipsley will be in attendance."

"Won't it be awkward for him if Gracie is present as well?" Sybil asked.

"Rotherham has ducked into the shadows with every unmarried woman present," Damaris reminded her. "There's no such thing as a ton gathering without half of the female guests being recipients of Rotherham's rakish advances."

"Technically," said Philippa, "he didn't actually kiss Gracie."

"In which case, she'll be the least potentially ruinous of the young ladies in attendance."

"Except for a small matter of a stolen tiara and a stolen hairpin," said Lady Eunice.

"Except for that," Damaris agreed. "Although Rotherham must realize Gracie cannot accuse him of stealing it without implicating herself for loose morals."

The front door to Lady Quarrington's house opened. Four smartly dressed ladies strolled down the path to the main road and turned toward the

Strathmore estate. Lady Quarrington, Philippa's mother, Theodosia, and Gracie.

"Off they go," said Florentia. "Other guests are already arriving."

Half of the seats encircling the rotunda had filled. The first trio of young ladies tuned their violins, then stood with their bows poised above the strings.

Lady Strathmore gave the sign.

Music filled the air, the bright melody of the first of Vivaldi's *Four Seasons*.

"Now?" whispered Sybil.

"Wait for Gracie and Theodosia to be given seats," Chloe murmured. "Lady Eunice, you have your violin. You can put your name on the list of performers. While Great-Aunt Wynchester is inside, we must keep everyone else outside."

Lady Eunice nodded. "I'll only begin playing if I need to send a warning. How about the key of B Major if you should move quickly, and the key of B Minor if you should take cover?"

"How about playing something that sounds like a warning?" Great-Aunt Wynchester said.

"Fair enough," said Lady Eunice. "I'll play Bach's *Chaconne* loud enough to be heard a mile away. It will definitely put all of the guests' attention on me, rather than you."

"I will search Lord Rotherham," Chloe said. "If the hairpin is on his person, I shall find it. Marjorie will guard his brother. Gracie will monopolize Lady Strathmore, should her attention stray from the musicians and her guests. Elizabeth, you shall deal with Lord Strathmore—"

Elizabeth held up her sword stick.

"Not like that," Philippa murmured.

"—whilst Great-Aunt Wynchester searches Rotherham's private quarters," Chloe finished.

"The open windows won't help," Sybil worried.

"Graham said half of Rotherham's windows face the garden party," Damaris added.

"The bedrooms are upstairs," said Great-Aunt Wynchester. "No one will be watching from the garden."

"The key is not to get caught," Chloe agreed.

"How will she not get caught, if the windows are open and facing the party?" Lady Eunice asked.

"What are twelve uninvited guests for, if not to cause a distraction?" Chloe replied. "With luck, everyone's attention will be riveted on whomever is performing. Should that not be the case... improvise."

"The guests are taking seats!" Florentia pointed.

Philippa pushed down her hand.

Footmen were hurriedly bringing out a few extra chairs to place near the hibiscus. Butterflies stirred in their wake.

"Lady Strathmore looks thrilled by the inconvenience," Sybil observed.

"She would have preferred to have planned it," Florentia said, "but if her intimate party turns into a major crush, Lady Strathmore will gain recognition as a much sought-after hostess."

Damaris grinned. "Ready to give her a major crush?"

The ladies turned to face each other.

Sybil cheered, "*Vive le Heist Club!*"

"Stop saying 'Heist Club,'" Philippa hissed. "In any language."

No one heard her over the sound of the others echoing Sybil's cheer.

The Wynchester ladies were already out of the belvedere and halfway to the road. Philippa and her friends followed at once.

Chloe pulled a thick shawl from her wicker basket and handed it to her aunt. Great-Aunt Wynchester immediately wrapped the shawl about her thin shoulders and prodigious bosom, which today somehow seemed even larger than Philippa remembered.

She imagined Great-Aunt Wynchester must have been stunning in her youth, with her fine bone structure. It was sweet to see Chloe taking such good care of her.

When they all reached the front door of the Strathmore residence, the butler's eyes widened, but he smoothly assured the ladies servants would be dispatched forthwith to carry extra chairs to the garden.

"Excellent," Great-Aunt Wynchester murmured. "Whilst all of the staff is outside, I shall be *in*side."

Whilst the butler's attention was upon a pair of footmen in the corridor behind him, Great-Aunt

Wynchester slipped around the far corner of the house, where the open windows were out of view of the party.

"If anyone asks, I'm in the retiring room," Philippa whispered to Damaris, then took off after Great-Aunt Wynchester.

She was finished being a bystander. Today, Philippa would have an important part.

Great-Aunt Wynchester turned toward the window in shock as Philippa hoisted herself over the sill into what appeared to be a dining room.

"What the devil do you think you're doing?"

"Helping," Philippa replied as she brushed off her skirts. "I'm the only one who has been inside this house before. You need me."

"And *you* need not to be caught sneaking in or out of Rotherham's bedchamber," Great-Aunt Wynchester replied. "If someone spies you, it will be an even bigger scandal. If you're believed to be one of his 'conquests,' you may even be forced to wed him."

"Then let's not be caught," said Philippa.

She skirted past the long table and peeked out of the open door into the corridor. There were no servants in sight.

"Follow me," she whispered.

Great-Aunt Wynchester made an aggravated noise, but followed close behind.

"—take chairs from the storage room," came a distant male voice.

Philippa and Great-Aunt Wynchester exchanged alarmed glances.

"*Here.*" Philippa grabbed Great-Aunt Wynchester's hand and tugged her down the corridor and in through the first unlocked door.

CHAPTER 10

"We're in a serving room," Great-Aunt Wynchester explained. "Graham was able to befriend a maid, so I have some idea of the layout. The stairs are to our right. Rotherham's private quarters are in the rear corner."

"Thank you," Philippa said. "For not pushing me right back out of that window."

"Don't get caught," Great-Aunt Wynchester muttered, and tilted her ear toward the door.

Footsteps and a murmur of voices sounded in the corridor as footmen carried the chairs out of the dining room and off to the garden.

When all was silent, Great-Aunt Wynchester eased open the door and doddered bewilderedly out into the corridor, looking for all the world as though she'd stumbled into this wing by mistake and had no idea where to go from here.

Then, in a blink, the confusion vanished from her

wrinkled face. Great-Aunt Wynchester was not nearly as dotty as she liked to appear. With one liver-spotted hand, she motioned for Philippa to follow her.

"If my footsteps don't creak, step where I step," Great-Aunt Wynchester whispered. "If they make noise, step somewhere else."

Philippa nodded her understanding.

The older woman led her to a set of stairs. They hurried up to the next floor. Great-Aunt Wynchester paused before heading down the corridor toward Rotherham's chambers.

"Mind the open windows," she murmured. "The trick now is to avoid maids *and* being seen from the garden."

"How will we do that?" Philippa said cautiously.

"By walking as though we're meant to be on this floor. Don't move so quickly as to catch the eye, nor slowly enough to be considered furtive. Match the pace of a chambermaid. The others may sense movement, but they won't notice us."

Match the pace of a chambermaid.

Had Philippa ever timed or properly analyzed the movements or pace of any servant in her home?

Great-Aunt Wynchester was right. Staff was seen, but not noticed. Philippa made a mental note to be more aware when she returned home.

Great-Aunt Wynchester set off down the corridor first. Philippa tried to mimic her.

It didn't work. Philippa's limbs felt clumsy. She

was suddenly too aware of her arms and legs and hands and feet. All of which took up far more space than they ought to.

When Great-Aunt Wynchester reached what was apparently the door to Rotherham's private chamber, she paused.

"When I turn the handle," the older woman murmured, "dash across the dressing room and close the curtains of the window to the left. I'll do the window on the right."

Philippa nodded. Her heart was pounding too quickly to allow her to form words. What if the door was locked? What if the door was *not* locked, and Rotherham's valet was inside? Her pulse skittered. Perhaps they *should* have brought Elizabeth and her sword stick.

"Ready?" Great-Aunt Wynchester whispered.

Philippa was not ready. She nodded anyway.

Great-Aunt Wynchester twisted the handle, pushed open the door, and sprinted toward the far window. This was clearly a dressing room, rather than a bedroom. There was a large dressing table, two armoires, and several mirrors hung throughout.

Philippa dashed to the opposite window, doing her best to stay out of sight. Dark clouds gathered overhead. The air seemed heavy as she slid the glass closed.

"Here. Pin the curtains closed." Great-Aunt Wynchester reached into her bosom and tossed something small through the air.

Philippa managed to catch the wooden clip. She considered saying, *You carry wooden pegs in your cleavage?* but obviously the answer was yes, and this was not the moment to argue the merits of reticules. She clasped the curtains together instead.

A murmur of female voices sounded in the corridor.

Great-Aunt Wynchester pulled a small wooden triangle from her ample bosom and wedged it beneath the door.

"We haven't a key to lock it," she explained, "but that should be enough to stop a maid from barging in."

Philippa nodded. She could not help but wonder what else hid beneath Great-Aunt Wynchester's shawl.

Already, the white-haired lady was moving to the connecting door. Philippa followed. Her heart wasn't banging as loudly this time. Lord Rotherham was out in the garden, and it was unlikely some lovestruck girl was awaiting him in his bedroom.

Wasn't it?

She held her breath as Great-Aunt Wynchester pushed open the door.

The bedroom was empty.

Philippa caught the flying clasp in her hand this time and hurried to secure the nearest windows.

"All right. Now, all we have left to do is..." Great-Aunt Wynchester turned in the center of the large, opulent chamber. "Locate a hairpin smaller than my little finger."

"Simple as I stand here," Philippa murmured. It was going to be impossible.

"Do you want to take the bedchamber or the dressing room?" Great-Aunt Wynchester asked.

"Er," Philippa said. "Dressing room?"

She'd rather avoid a rake's bed.

Great-Aunt Wynchester gave a sharp nod. "You have ten minutes."

"*Ten minutes?*" Philippa stared at her. "To search an entire dressing room?"

"Don't look where the hairpin *isn't*," Great-Aunt Wynchester said patiently. "Look in the places where a stolen hairpin is most likely to *be*."

Of course. Why hadn't Philippa considered skipping all of the wrong places and jumping straight to *et voilà?*

It wasn't as though there would be an enormous arrow with a sign reading, "Stolen hairpin over here."

Great-Aunt Wynchester had already turned away to begin her search. "Nine minutes."

Philippa hastened to the dressing room and sent a frantic gaze about the room. There was an armoire, a dressing table and chair, a plethora of mirrors, a beautiful tub, a side table with basin and pitcher...

Should she begin with the armoire? If Rotherham kept the pin on his person, Chloe might have already found it.

Or, he might have accidentally left it pinned to a prior item of clothing, such as last night's frock coat.

She opened the armoire and began feeling through the folded clothing.

No, this was silly. Rotherham might be careless enough to leave a stolen hairpin clasped to his lapel, but his valet would surely have noticed.

And then what? Returned it to a jewelry chest?

She closed the armoire and turned back to the dressing table.

Its mahogany surface contained an ornate hand mirror, several candles, a portable writing slope... and something that might be a small jewelry chest.

She hurried over to and lifted the lid.

Rings, cravat pins, an eye miniature that might or might not depict Miss Ipsley...

No hairpin.

"*Damn* it," Philippa muttered. Her frustration reflected back at her in the dressing table's gilt-edged mirror, as did the inscription engraved on the portable desk—

Furtivus thesaurus

Philippa blinked. So there *was* a sign pointing straight to the hairpin.

"Mrs. Wynchester?" she called softly. "I think I found it."

The older woman was at her side in seconds. "Where?"

Philippa pointed at the writing slope.

Great-Aunt Wynchester's wrinkled brow creased even more. "The letters are backward."

"It's clear in the mirror."

"Not to me." Great-Aunt Wynchester opened the slope and poked around inside. "What does the engraving say?"

"'Stolen treasures,'" Philippa quoted.

"You must be bamming me." Great-Aunt Wynchester moved everything from the writing slope to the dressing table. "Why would a thief make it obvious where to find his stolen contraband?"

Philippa frowned. "He wouldn't."

By all accounts, Lord Rotherham didn't even speak Latin. It was his brother who prided himself on his command of the Classics.

Great-Aunt Wynchester shook the empty slope. It rattled. She flipped it over to reveal a second compartment. "This had better not contain more ink and plumes and parchment."

When she opened the lid, a dazzling hoard of women's jewelry glittered back at them. Earrings and brooches and hair combs and lockets.

Philippa and Great-Aunt Wynchester exchanged startled glances.

"Stolen treasures indeed," Philippa murmured.

"We *must* talk to the other ladies. Today, before we leave the party."

They couldn't leave the stolen items behind, nor could they walk out of the house carrying Lord Rotherham's writing slope. Where was Chloe and her omnipresent basket when one needed them?

"The good news," said Great-Aunt Wynchester as she lifted an aigrette, "is I think we found the hairpin."

"The bad news," said Philippa, "is that we're going to need a bigger reticule."

CHAPTER 11

A discordant melody rose from the garden below, as if one of the violinists had suddenly decided to play an entirely different arrangement than the rest.

Great-Aunt Wynchester's eyes met Philippa's.

"Lady Eunice," they said in unison.

Philippa ran to the window and peeked through the side edge of the curtains.

"*Blast*. It started to sprinkle." She turned from the glass, her heart pounding. "Only a few ladies are carrying umbrellas or parasols. At any moment, the entire party could come inside. Marjorie is physically blocking Mr. Briggs, and Elizabeth just took her cane and... We must make haste before we're caught coming down the stairs."

Great-Aunt Wynchester tossed her shawl to the dressing table. "Retrieve the curtain clips from the other room while I confiscate the stolen jewelry."

Philippa *meant* to follow instructions, and *would* have followed instructions, had Great-Aunt Wynchester not then lowered her bodice and removed her ponderous bosom.

"You wear false *breasts?*" Philippa blurted out.

"Where else would I keep my collection of clips and wedges?" Great-Aunt Wynchester replied reasonably.

The false bosom appeared to be fashioned out of papier-mâché and then covered with a thick layer of wool on the outside. A burlap bag lined the interior of each hollow breast, with a drawstring to keep it closed.

Great-Aunt Wynchester wasted no time in filling the sacks with the spoils from Rotherham's writing slope.

She was adding the last pieces when Philippa returned with the curtain clips.

"I recognize that brooch," Philippa said in surprise. "And those earrings—I could swear they belong to young women here at this party."

"He appears to have nicked jewels from half of the ladies in the ton," said Great-Aunt Wynchester as she re-affixed her false bosom beneath her bodice.

Outdoors, the music stopped all at once.

Murmurs and shouts filled the air, along with the unmistakable sound of a sudden downpour.

Philippa's limbs froze. "They're fleeing inside. *At this very moment.*"

"Come along, then," Great-Aunt Wynchester said briskly. "We've done as we meant to do."

The older woman scooped the wooden wedge up from beneath the door and tucked it into her papier-mâché cleavage before wrapping her shawl back around her shoulders, hiding the evidence from sight.

"Shut the windows!" came a call from the other side of the door.

"I'll close the other side!" came the answering reply from further down the hall.

Great-Aunt Wynchester eased open the door, then quickly shut it. "Shite."

"What is it?" Philippa asked in alarm.

"Rotherham's valet." The older woman glanced about the room. "Under the bed? No—dirt and dust on our clothes would be too difficult to explain away. We'll have to… *Here.*" She grabbed Philippa's hand and pulled her into one of the large armoires.

There were too many clothes. Philippa felt as though she was being smothered by cambric and silk. Great-Aunt Wynchester pulled the armoire shut seconds before they heard the dressing room door open.

"I've got this room," called a muffled male voice.

Either he didn't move, or his footsteps were silent against the thick carpet.

Great-Aunt Wynchester's hand was still holding Philippa's. It did not feel papery, but soft, except for a few calloused fingertips. What were the older woman's hobbies? Rope-climbing and blacksmithing?

She also had a distinct smell. Not the one Philippa associated with her own grandparents, but more like… citrus and leather. *Pomade.* Great-Aunt Wynchester smelt of pomade. Rich and expensive and completely bizarre, just like the rest of the family.

Then again, Great-Aunt Wynchester possessed a prodigious amount of white hair. Philippa could only imagine the quantity of pins and wax necessary to keep that much thick hair from succumbing to gravity. Why not smell nice while she was at it?

"Humph," came the valet's muffled voice. "I told those girls not to touch my lord's rooms. Impertinent maids. Always going where they oughtn't and…"

The dressing room door closed and his words were no longer audible.

Philippa started to push open the armoire door, but Great-Aunt Wynchester tightened her hold on Philippa's hand.

"Give it a moment," she murmured. "*We* know the maids haven't overstepped in this instance, but they might come and take a peek now that the valet has gone."

Philippa nodded, then remembered Great-Aunt Wynchester couldn't see her in the dark. "I like your pomade," she whispered.

Great-Aunt Wynchester was silent for a long moment before responding. "I meant to wash it out."

"I'm glad you didn't. I can't quite put my finger on the citrus—"

"Bergamot."

"That's it. Bergamot. It's lovely in tea. And pomade, I gather."

"Don't tease, pip. Wait until you're my age. Old ladies will do anything to capture a shade of our former beauty."

"You're still quite beautiful," Philippa assured her. Wrinkled, yes. Liver-spotted, yes. Hunched and hobbling, yes. But nothing could disguise the handsome woman Great-Aunt Wynchester had once been. "When I am your age, I hope not to care what people think of me at all."

"You can begin now," Great-Aunt Wynchester suggested. "I rather thought you already had."

"Oh, I'm not like you," Philippa murmured. "I…"

…am holding hands with an octogenarian whilst hiding in an armoire.

"You may have a point," she admitted. "I care very much what my friends think, and even more what my parents think, but I did choose my small group of bluestockings over the company of—"

"—my darling Philippa!" came a distant voice, loud enough to be heard down the corridor and through the door.

Mother.

Philippa tried to disappear into Rotherham's clothing.

"Now, madam, you know she's not up here, and

neither should you be," one of the maids said loudly. "Come with me, if you please, madam, and I'll take you to the others."

"But my daughter isn't with the others! Something has happened to her. If Rotherham has taken illicit liberties, he *will* marry her, you mark my words—"

"We're done up here," said the other maid. "I'll help you escort the nice lady back to her friends."

"That was a near miss," Great-Aunt Wynchester whispered. "If she'd caught us together, we'd have been forced to marry."

Philippa chuckled at the image. It was impossible to imagine what her mother—or anyone—would think to find a very proper bluestocking and her very improper chaperone squished up against several dozen shirts and waistcoats.

"I think it's safe to peek." Great-Aunt Wynchester dropped Philippa's hand and eased open the armoire door. They were met with silence. She stepped out and hobbled to the dressing room door, then bent to peer through the keyhole. "Empty. This is our chance. All the same, act like we belong, but are in a hurry."

Great-Aunt Wynchester pulled open the door and strode down the corridor.

Philippa didn't even breathe until her feet were back on the ground floor. They were still far from the front parlor, however.

And footsteps were coming in their direction. *Lots*

of footsteps.

"In here." Great-Aunt Wynchester opened a door and hurried Philippa inside.

Philippa's shoulders relaxed when she realized where they were. The music room was often used to host parties during inclement weather. Even if that wasn't the plan for today, their presence in a common public room like this would not be the disaster getting caught upstairs would have been.

Of course, they hadn't actually *attended* the party...

Great-Aunt Wynchester hurried toward the window, keeping a protective hand over her cloaked bodice. "I'll call Zeus."

Now was the right time to summon an old, wet Mastiff with a snuffbox chained to his collar?

Philippa parted the curtains. The window had been closed. The retreating garden party was on the opposite side of the house.

Great-Aunt Wynchester opened the window several inches and gave a respectable robin call.

Zeus bounded up to the window. The unopenable wooden barrel hung from his harness.

"Perfect." Great-Aunt Wynchester relieved Zeus of the barrel, patted his head, and shut the window. "That ought to do the trick."

"What trick?" Philippa blurted out. "At any moment, the entire party shall burst through that door. They didn't see us outside, so they won't be expecting to find us on the inside. What possible excuse—"

The door opened.

A stream of footmen flooded into the room, each appearing slightly sprinkled-upon. Upon seeing two unexpected women inside of the music room, the footmen stopped in their tracks.

This caused the river of guests in the corridor to likewise crash together.

A thin, pale hand rose behind the bobbing heads and made strangely emphatic gestures.

"Briggs," Great-Aunt Wynchester muttered.

Philippa stared at her. There was no possibility of that tiny hand belonging to—

Mr. Briggs elbowed his way through the guests and across the threshold. "How did you get in here before me?"

"*Eh?*" Great-Aunt Wynchester quavered, squinting as she doddered forward. "If you're speaking to me, pup, you'd be best served not to mumble."

"*Pup?*" Mr. Briggs spluttered. "Who *is* this woman, and what is she doing in our house? As if bluestockings weren't troublesome enough—"

Philippa did her best to mimic how she'd seen Chloe react in similar circumstances.

"This is Great-Aunt Wynchester," Philippa said brightly, as if this were the most obvious and normal turn of events that might have transpired.

"We came indoors before it started to rain. These old joints can sense rain long before you green bucks could spot a cloud with an opera glass," Great-Aunt Wynchester quavered, shaking a liver-spotted fist. "One ought not to throw garden parties in a deluge, I always say."

"I never saw you *at* the party!" Mr. Briggs turned to Philippa. "I saw your mother, Miss York, but I did not see you."

"Of *course* you didn't see her, pup!' said Great-Aunt Wynchester. "How could you see her, when we were busy rescuing the wildlife fleeing your garden? If you'd kept your eyes on the shrubbery rather than your pretty violinists, perhaps you'd have a clue what was happening around you."

"Keep eyes on... shrubbery..." Mr. Briggs goggled at her. "*What* wildlife?"

By now, Lady Strathmore and dozens of other guests had pressed their way into the music room.

The Duchess of Faircliffe swept to the front.

"Why, Great-Aunt Wynchester, there you are," Chloe said warmly, as if this was precisely where she'd been planning to meet her aunt all along. "Did you catch them?"

"I did," Great-Aunt Wynchester said with pride.

She held the small wooden barrel aloft and popped the two halves apart as if they barely stuck together.

Philippa started. "How did you...?"

The question was immediately forgotten as confused butterflies fluttered free from the dark barrel, flapping their wings higher as they soared above the heads of the guests gathered in the music room. Philippa's eyes met Great-Aunt Wynchester's, and they shared a private grin.

"Oooh," cooed the crowd, rushing past them to gaze up at the butterflies.

"*Now*," whispered Great-Aunt Wynchester, as she hooked her arm through Philippa's.

CHAPTER 12

Great-Aunt Wynchester pulled Philippa closer to Chloe. After bumping into the duchess—literally—the older woman latched onto Chloe instead of Philippa and whispered something into Chloe's ear.

Rather than respond aloud, the duchess dropped her arm from her aunt's and turned to the party's hostess, Lady Strathmore.

"We shall continue the performance in here," said Lady Strathmore. "Until the weather improves."

"But first," suggested Chloe, "perhaps it's best to divide the party into separate withdrawing rooms long enough to allow pulses to settle and bodies to refresh after all of this excitement."

Philippa held her breath. As a duchess, Chloe outranked a countess. However, this was Lady Strathmore's home, not Chloe's.

The countess surveyed the chaotic music room with obvious distraction.

"I suppose you're right," she said at last. "The men can have port in the dining room, and the ladies can reconvene in the front parlor whilst the musicians have a moment to collect themselves here and prepare for the next performance."

"Wonderful idea," said Chloe, as though it had been Lady Strathmore who had thought of it. "As the ladies far outnumber the gentlemen—"

This was not Lady Strathmore's fault, but rather a consequence of Philippa's reading circle descending upon the party unexpectedly.

"—perhaps it will be best to have the younger set in the yellow sitting room, whilst the elder generation takes advantage of your truly delightful parlor. My aunt has offered to chaperone the young ladies—"

"*Your* aunt?" Lady Strathmore choked. "Lead *my* guests?"

"I told her it was nonsense," Chloe assured the countess. "*You* are the hostess. Of course you shall preside over the grand parlor. Miss York has kindly offered to settle the young ladies in the sitting room."

"Er, yes." Philippa straightened. "That's exactly what I said."

"Well... I suppose," said Lady Strathmore. "You *did* bring most of them with you."

Philippa's cheeks flushed. She was not used to

acting outside of convention. Or traveling amongst large groups of friends.

She rather liked it.

"Would it help if I informed the guests?" Chloe asked.

"No, no," said Lady Strathmore. "It's my idea; I'll tell them."

"As you wish," Chloe murmured.

Lady Strathmore clapped her hands together and made the announcement to the crowd. Refreshments would be served to the three separate groups, after which the concert would resume here in the music room.

"Aren't you just an angel," cooed Elizabeth Wynchester, leaning heavily on her cane. "A moment to collect myself will be just the thing."

Lady Strathmore inclined her head regally. "I always look after my guests."

In short order, the occupants of the music room dispersed into their assigned areas, gentlemen to the dining room, the older generation to the parlor, and the younger ladies to the yellow sitting room.

Well, the younger ladies and Great-Aunt Wynchester.

Philippa hurried to join Gracie and Theodosia. "We have your pin."

Theodosia nearly toppled over in relief.

"Thank you," Gracie gushed. "*Thank you.*"

"Actually," whispered Philippa, "we have far more than your hairpin. Lord Rotherham has been at this game for some time. He pilfered trinkets from countless young ladies, several of whom are here in this parlor."

Gracie's mouth fell open. "That *scoundrel*."

Theodosia gripped Philippa's arm. "We must return every stolen object and prevent him from undertaking such dastardly behavior again."

"We will," Philippa promised, although she wasn't yet certain how they would achieve such a thing.

She moved to stand closer to Chloe and Great-Aunt Wynchester.

Elizabeth closed the door to the sitting room and leaned against it.

"Do it now," she said, "before the kitchen has a chance to prepare tea."

The other young ladies looked at each other in confusion.

Chloe lifted the lid of her wicker basket and pulled out two bulging burlap bags.

"You slipped her your *breasts?*" Philippa whispered to Great-Aunt Wynchester. "When? How?"

Great-Aunt Wynchester peeked under her shawl. "I think she took them when I wasn't looking."

Miss Ipsley made a loud sniff across the room. "I hope this isn't a ham-fisted attempt to force us into your little reading circle. Now that you bluestockings have trapped us away from the party, pray tell us what you want."

"To help you," said Chloe, her tone impressively calm. "The scandal columns have accused several women in this room of cavorting wantonly with rakish Lord Rotherham."

Half a dozen faces blushed bright pink.

"What I'd like to know," Chloe continued, "is how many of you later discovered yourself to be missing an accessory?"

Murmurs filled the sitting room.

"A brooch," said Miss Pugh tentatively.

"Earrings," said Miss Oglethorpe.

"I didn't even kiss him," said Miss Agnew. "But I couldn't say so without admitting I'd been alone with him, for how else would he be in possession of my hair comb?"

"I didn't kiss him either," Miss Pugh said in surprise.

Miss Oglethorpe's jaw fell open. "Nor I."

"If you would like your jewelry back, you're in luck." Chloe upended the contents of both bags atop a crimson chaise longue.

Gasps filled the room.

"My earrings!" cried Miss Oglethorpe as she dashed to rescue them.

Miss Pugh burst into tears at the sight of her lost brooch. "I have been living in a fog of fear, knowing my reputation could be ruined at any moment!"

"Does anyone recognize any of the other jewelry?" Philippa asked. "We need to return every item to its owner."

"I do," said Miss Agnew. "That locket clearly belongs to—"

THE RAKE MISTAKE

All of the ladies started talking over each other at once as they identified each piece and whom it belonged to.

Chloe took furious notes in Graham Wynchester's journal.

Miss Ipsley's face was pale. "I cannot believe Rotherham has become so awful. To think I fancied myself still in love with the blackguard!"

"Shall we instigate legal proceedings?" Philippa asked.

"*No,*" all of the affected ladies said at once.

"We cannot admit the circumstances of the theft," pleaded Miss Overton.

"I'll admit mine," Gracie said bravely. "If it will help all of you."

"No one's reputation is getting ruined," barked Great-Aunt Wynchester. "Except Lord Rotherham's. I shall fetch him for a reckoning at once."

"Fetch him," gasped Miss Pugh. "And cause a public scandal?"

"He will be embarrassed only in front of the people in this room," Chloe pointed out. "The society matrons are having tea in the other wing."

Miss Ipsley's voice shook. "We must shame him into never acting this way again."

Elizabeth moved aside so Great-Aunt Wynchester could open the door.

"Bring Mr. Briggs," Philippa called out.

All eyes turned to look at her.

"Rotherham's younger brother?" Miss Agnew asked in confusion. "Whatever for?"

"I'm not certain yet," Philippa admitted, "but I'll wager he's involved up to his eyeballs."

In no time, Great-Aunt Wynchester tottered back into the room, with an equally bewildered gentleman attached to each elbow.

Elizabeth shut the door and leaned against it.

"Explain yourself!" Great-Aunt Wynchester demanded.

"Explain... what?" asked Lord Rotherham, baffled.

"Why you hid stolen treasures in a container labeled 'stolen treasures,'" Philippa said tartly.

Lord Rotherham's sculpted cheekbones flushed red... and then drained of blood.

"Marked... 'stolen treasures'? But the only person who knew was…" Rotherham whirled to face his brother. "*You* had my writing slope engraved after that poetry circle. You told me it said, 'Born romantic and future poet!'"

"You should have learnt to read Latin." Mr. Briggs sneered. "It wasn't even written in the right direction, you fool. I don't know *what* she sees in you."

Philippa's mouth fell open. "You mean... Miss Ipsley?"

"Me?" squeaked Miss Ipsley. "What has any of this to do with *me*?"

Lord Rotherham threw himself on his knees at her feet. "You said you would only marry a man unafraid to go after what he wanted. I wanted to prove to you I was as confident as any rake, but I couldn't bear to fully go through with it. The only person I've ever wished to kiss was you."

"What I meant," said Miss Ipsley, "was that if you wanted to marry me, then you ought to *ask* me! We shared dozens of waltzes and you sent one hundred poems, yet you never once said it was anything more than a flirtation."

"I said so in every one of those hundred poems," Lord Rotherham protested, pressing her hands to his chest. "Your lips ignite my ardor like—"

Mr. Briggs groaned theatrically. "Spare us your inferior poetry, brother. If your poems were any good, she would have got your meaning before you set about terrorizing the ton as a make-believe rake."

"But how would they know?" asked Rotherham, his face lined with confusion. "I was going to give the jewelry back as soon as I won Miss Ipsley's hand. In the meantime, I took great pains to hide those trinkets out of sight."

"Inside a writing slope labeled 'stolen treasures,'" Philippa reminded him.

She could see the moment in Rotherham's eyes when he reasoned it out.

He leapt to his feet and rounded on his brother. "*You* gossiped to the scandal columns?"

"She didn't want you," Mr. Briggs burst out. "All your antics were doing was driving her away. If poetry was enough to win her over, *mine* would have done so. But no, she was still infatuated with *you*—"

Rotherham sputtered, "You sent poetry to Miss Ipsley?"

"Dreadful poems," Miss Ipsley murmured. "Full of Latin. Yours were much better. Even if you are an idiot."

"An idiot in love with you," said Lord Rotherham. "Is it too late to beg for your hand?"

Miss Ipsley placed her hand in his. "Ask me and see."

"Oh, for the love of..." Mr. Briggs turned toward the door.

Elizabeth pulled the serpent's head hilt from her cane, revealing a wicked blade.

"By the way," called Chloe, as she ran her finger down a page in Graham's journal, "I received word this morning that a Mr. Briggs has been disinvited from his poetry circle."

Mr. Briggs's eyes popped.

From her position, Philippa could see that the line Chloe was pointing at in her journal was completely blank. Nonetheless, Philippa had no doubt the Wynchesters would make the claim true in the time it took Mr. Briggs to stomp off.

"You're my brother," said Lord Rotherham. "Yet you tried to steal the affection of the woman I love."

Mr. Briggs stared back at him stonily.

"You *encouraged* me to play the rake." Rotherham's cheeks flushed. "You said stealing those trinkets would ensure their silence. But it was *you* who tried to implicate me in scandal—and nearly ruined the lives of innocent young ladies in the process. I shall spend the rest of my days repenting for my part in this foolishness. You and I both must apologize to each and every one of them."

"You cannot order me about," Mr. Briggs blustered in high affront. "You are not the earl!"

"I will be," Lord Rotherham said quietly. "And unless you wish for me to come clean to our father, leaving no detail unconfessed..."

Mr. Briggs ground his teeth, then whirled toward the door.

This time, Elizabeth stood aside and let him pass.

"You *rotter*." Miss Oglethorpe's voice shook. "Do you know how worried I was when—"

"Worried?" Gracie blurted out. "I was terrified. That pin belonged to my sister."

"My necklace—"

"My grandmother's earrings—"

"My bracelet—"

"I'm sorry." Rotherham's eyes widened as if he were just now realizing the gravity of his actions. Pilfering an heirloom wasn't a harmless prank. It wasn't even simple theft of an object. These women had feared for their reputations and their futures. "I realize words are insufficient. I have behaved abominably. Tell me what I must do to put this right, and I will do it."

The ladies talked over one another with suggestions ranging from donating time to charitable causes, to Rotherham throwing himself in the closest river.

He nodded. "You're right. All of you. I should never have listened to my brother. I was so love-mad that I was willing to try anything to catch the eye of... But of course I don't deserve you." He collapsed to his knees at Miss Ipsley's feet. "I have never deserved you. What would you want with a swain as wretched as I?"

All eyes swung to Miss Ipsley.

"I'm sorry, ladies and bluestockings," she said, "for my unwitting role in this dreadful charade."

"It wasn't your fault," Gracie said. "We all followed him willingly."

"But my heart never strayed." Lord Rotherham bowed his head to Miss Ipsley's knees, then jerked his gaze up toward hers, his face tortured. "Can you see it in your heart to forgive a lovesick dunce who promises to spend the rest of his life making up for his past transgressions to you and everyone else he has so foolishly wronged?"

"It's a trick," Great-Aunt Wynchester warned her. "Some men aren't worth the bother."

Miss Ipsley touched Lord Rotherham's cheek. "This one might be. If he spends the rest of his life proving himself to be a much better man."

He kissed her hands and pressed them to his chest. "I shall become the most honorable man and most devoted suitor the ton has ever seen."

Philippa doubted *that*, but then again, she was a

bluestocking in possession of bookshelves and an imagination. It was clear Miss Ipsley had already made up her mind. Rotherham had proven himself more roguish than ever, but in a way that increased Miss Ipsley's sense of worth. They would be the most fashionable pair in the beau monde, and for a while, the most talked about. She supposed there were worse ways to find a husband.

More importantly, all of the stolen jewelry would now return where it belonged.

CHAPTER 13

Philippa, the Wynchesters, and the reading circle tossed sticks to Zeus in Lady Quarrington's garden.

The old Mastiff lumbered up to each stick without urgency, but with an abundance of good cheer. He had been a very, very, good boy, all of the ladies informed him between belly rubs. The butterflies had arrived right when they needed them.

"May I see the barrel?" asked Damaris.

"It's impossible to open," Chloe warned.

"Great-Aunt Wynchester opened it," Philippa said.

Great-Aunt Wynchester smiled.

"It's a puzzle," Elizabeth explained. "Each of the little wooden slats moves somehow, and if they're in just the right position, the locking mechanism disengages and the two halves come apart."

"I wish we had one for brandy," Lady Eunice said with a sigh.

Chloe opened the lid of her wicker basket. She tossed the wooden barrel to Damaris and handed Lady Eunice a small flask.

"You carry brandy in your basket?" Philippa asked.

"It's not brandy," Great-Aunt Wynchester murmured. "It's gin for improving bad orgeat. Watch Lady Eunice's face when she realizes."

Lady Eunice spluttered, then made a considering expression, then smiled and took a daintier sip.

"Ha!" crowed Damaris, holding two halves of the barrel aloft as though showing off the spoils of a hunt.

"*Impossible*," Chloe breathed. "How did she do that so quickly?"

"There's no use asking," said Florentia.

"She probably doesn't know," Sybil explained. "When it comes to puzzles and ciphers, Damaris is incredibly talented."

At the sound of her name, Damaris grinned and tossed the closed barrel to Florentia.

"Where are Gracie and Theodosia?" Elizabeth asked.

"They're already on their way back to London," Philippa answered. "Theodosia's reputation and marriage are no longer in jeopardy, and her betrothed is awaiting an explanation. Then Gracie is accompanying her sister for the final fitting of the bridal gown."

Sybil's eyes sparkled. "Theodosia will be wearing both hairpins to the wedding."

"The Wynchesters did it," said Lady Eunice. "And Philippa."

"You were all wonderful," Damaris said with a happy sigh.

Florentia turned to the Wynchesters. "Perhaps we could be an important resource to your family in future missions."

Lady Eunice returned the flask. "We can spread the word and find you new cases!"

Elizabeth buffed her cane. "Perhaps refrain from sharing details about legally questionable exploits among your circles in the beau monde."

"We prefer to help those who have no other recourse," Chloe explained.

"And we," said Sybil, "are here to help you help them every step of the way. The first rule of Heist Club is—"

"*Stop talking about Heist Club.*" Philippa threw up her hands. "That is the *only* rule."

The side door to Lady Quarrington's house opened and Philippa's mother emerged.

Chloe whistled to Zeus and attached the rope to his collar.

Mother approached with no tea trays and her chin held high.

"The party is over," she announced. "You may all return home."

Lady Eunice's eyes widened in surprise. "Lady Strathmore canceled the 'welcome home' gala?"

"No, there's still a gala. It is now a *betrothal party*." Mother pronounced the words as if each syllable were poisonous. "We shall not be attending. There is no point to it anymore." She turned to Philippa and hissed, "I said, 'Flirt with him', not 'Matchmake him to someone else.'"

"They wanted to marry each other long before *I* arrived," Philippa said. "They're in love."

"Bah," scoffed her mother. "One would think Lady Strathmore would raise her sons with more sense than to fall in love. Rotherham could have had *you*."

Philippa was very grateful that he did not.

"Mark my words," said her mother. "I'll have you married off the moment the London season begins anew. Don't even dream of defying me next time. You'll never see your boring Bluestocking Brigade again."

Sybil straightened. "We're the Hei—"

Damaris clapped a hand over Sybil's mouth.

"Be in the carriage in twenty minutes," said Mother. "Your trunks are being loaded now."

With that, she turned on her heel and stalked back into Lady Quarrington's house.

An uneasy silence filled the garden.

"It's nothing," Philippa assured her friends. "I've been a 'devastating disappointment' since birth, and despaired of finding the trick of making my parents happy. Apparently, all I must do is accept whomever they force to marry me. It will be fine."

"It sounds horrid," Damaris muttered.

"Well, yes," Philippa admitted. "I've no doubt my impending union will be dreadful." It didn't matter. It was what she had been raised to do. "Mother doesn't believe in love. I'm not certain I do either."

"How can you say that?" gasped Lady Eunice. "Theodosia was utterly destroyed at the thought of losing her beloved."

Philippa tried to explain. "I believe love exists for people like Theodosia and Miss Ipsley. But I've never felt that spark. What if there's no one out there who could feel it for me?"

The door to the house flung open. "Philippa! Ten minutes!"

As Chloe adjusted Great-Aunt Wynchester's shawl, she whispered, "You should tell her."

Great-Aunt Wynchester cleared her throat, hesitated, then shook her head.

Philippa leaned forward. "Tell me what?"

∽

Romance, adventure, and a wee heist or two await Miss Philippa when the Wynchesters reveal their secrets in The Perks of Loving a Wallflower!

. . .

How did Chloe steal Philippa's fiancé? (Er, besides literally. Whilst commandeering his carriage.) Find out in The Duke Heist!

Want more Heist Club capers featuring the Wild Wynchesters and their plucky bluestocking sidekicks? Join the VIP list at https://ridley.vip to be invited on future capers!

ACKNOWLEDGMENTS

As always, I could not have written this book without the invaluable support of my critique partner, beta readers, and editors. Huge thanks go out to Rose Lerner and Erica Monroe. You are the best! Special thanks to Olivia Waite, for the much-appreciated assist with Latin. All mistakes are my own.

I took a bit of artistic license and used the words "heist" and "caper" prior to their first recorded usage. I hope you forgive the indulgence. I loved the joke and adore the ladies of the reading circle, and I hope you do, too.

I also want to thank my wonderful VIP readers, our Historical Romance Book Club on Facebook, and my fabulous early reader team. Your enthusiasm makes the romance happen.

Thank you so much!

THE PERKS OF LOVING A WALLFLOWER

❦

PRIVATE ARC

CHAPTER 1

October 1817
London, England

Tommy Wynchester strolled off one of the many boats docked at Billingsgate and melted into the marketplace. The smell of the water permeated the crisp air, as did the cacophony of voices, punctuated by the cries of vendors hawking fish, crabs, and countless other treats and treasures.

It was the perfect place for a boatman to disappear.

From the busy stalls clustered along the dock, a gentleman emerged. The brim of his hat was pulled down low against the chill autumn wind, but Tommy didn't need to see his face to recognize him. Tall and rugged. Black hair and bronze skin. An annoying habit of quoting dramatically from the morning scandal columns when one was trying to eat one's breakfast.

"You got it?" Graham murmured when their elbows were close enough to touch.

"Of course." She slid him the package.

He continued on.

In moments, Tommy's brother had vanished into the milling crowd, slipperier than the eels hawked beside the water. He might have a horse tied to a post somewhere under guard. Or he might scale the brick in a narrow alleyway, choosing to race across rooftops instead of slog through the congested street traffic.

Tommy's part in the mission was over. She could relax and give up the life of a boatman. And she knew just where to begin: the Clams & Cockles Inn.

Two women sat in wicker chairs at Tommy's favorite table overlooking the water. The diminutive blond one with the faraway expression and the clumps of red paint in her hair was Tommy's sister Marjorie. The woman with the sharp green eyes and a sturdy sword stick was Tommy's sister Elizabeth.

The only one missing was Chloe.

Tommy and Chloe had been inseparable from the moment they'd met at the orphanage. Tommy had been little more than a toddler. They'd grown up together, first as orphans with side-by-side cots and then as wards of the eccentric Baron Vanderbean.

But Chloe had married a duke. She had new responsibilities and was no longer free to join in her siblings' exploits, no matter how much Tommy missed her.

"Where are they?" she asked as she took her seat.

"Any minute now." Elizabeth's fingers caressed a brass handle in the shape of a serpent.

"Your oysters!" sang out a lusty voice. A serving girl placed a brimming basket in the center of the table, along with a tankard of ale for Tommy.

"You are the best sisters," Tommy said fervently, and reached for the oysters.

"And you're the worst," Elizabeth grumbled. "I wish *I* could swill pints of ale in public without receiving disapproving looks from passersby."

"Hit them with your sword stick," Marjorie suggested. "Judging strangers is rude."

"Or become a boatman," Tommy said between bites, careful to face her sister when she spoke. It was difficult for Marjorie to hear over the noise of a crowd. "No one pays any mind to what we do."

"You are not a boatman," Elizabeth reminded her. "You are playing a role."

"*Were* playing," Marjorie corrected, her voice loud and pointed.

Tommy's many temporary roles did feel like playing a game. She loved each while it lasted, but was always glad to remove her costume and be herself.

"Did you find the fish spinster of your dreams?" Elizabeth asked.

"I was working," Tommy reminded her. "There will be time to look for love later."

"Liar," Elizabeth said. "You stopped looking the moment you laid eyes on—"

"Shush." Tommy felt her neck flush. "Wynchesters meddle in *other* people's business. Not mine."

Marjorie brightened. "And Graham?"

Relieved by the change in topic, Tommy waved her hand toward the buildings on the other side of the market. "He's off saving the day. Tonight, a father will finally reunite with his family. Thank you for the forgery, by the way."

"Always my pleasure," Marjorie replied primly.

"I could have gone on the boat with you," said Elizabeth. "I could have bludgeoned villains or poked holes in them with my blade."

"No poking necessary," Tommy assured her. "I would have signaled if we needed you."

"The signal wasn't badgers this time, was it?" Marjorie asked.

Tommy shook her head. "Polecats."

"Polecats," Marjorie repeated. "Should I ask, or is it better for me to remain in blissful ignorance?"

"Blissful ignorance," Elizabeth answered with feeling. "I don't even want to know how Jacob managed to *train* a polecat."

Each of the Wynchesters possessed unique talents that helped them to aid the downtrodden and the desperate. The siblings' methods might have been unorthodox…or at times a wee bit illegal…but at the end of the day, faith was restored to those who had lost hope, and justice was served.

What could work up a better appetite than that?

"Do you ever tire of being someone new?" Marjorie asked.

"Never," Tommy answered without hesitation.

She loved the cool wind whipping through her short brown hair and the cozy warmth of the linen cravat tied about her neck. She also adored swinging a heavy hammer at an anvil, blustering along as a myopic old woman, or mincing about as a helpless maiden.

Two decades ago, as a skinny six-year-old girl lying in a narrow cot in an orphanage, Tommy had dreamed about what sort of person she might become or what post she might hold when she grew up.

She never imagined the answer would be *all* of them!

One summer, rich, reclusive Baron Vanderbean had plucked six orphans from poverty and turned them into a family. He had given them a new direction and changed their lives forever.

It had been fifteen months since Bean had died. Tommy still missed him every day. But the Wynchester siblings carried on, doing their part to improve the lives of others, the way Bean had once done for them.

"What role haven't you played?" asked Marjorie.

"Prince Regent," Elizabeth said before Tommy could answer. "*That* I'd like to see."

"Or a princess," suggested Marjorie. "You have so many pretty wigs. You'd make a fetching Balcovian heiress."

"Pah," said Tommy. "I had my fill of flirting with fops and aristocrats the night of my wretched come-out ball." Proper debutante Miss Thomasina had been Tommy's *least* favorite role. One she would not be reprising. "I feel sorry for Chloe having to be the Duchess of Faircliffe now, poor thing. I would never mingle with Polite Society for fun."

Elizabeth's smile was wicked. "Not for…anyone?"

Tommy popped an oyster into her mouth to avoid responding.

"She would," Marjorie whispered to Elizabeth.

"I know she would," Elizabeth whispered back. "If a certain someone asked her to."

Tommy glared at them both, unable to snap *I can hear you talking about me* without likewise showing herself capable of responding to her meddling sisters' impertinent opinions.

She ate another oyster instead.

Elizabeth and Marjorie exchanged smug grins, as if Tommy had bared her soul.

THANK YOU

AND SNEAK PEEKS

THANK YOU FOR READING

Love talking books with fellow readers?

Join the *Historical Romance Book Club* for prizes, books, and live chats with your favorite romance authors:
    Facebook.com/groups/HistRomBookClub

And check out the official website for sneak peeks and more:
    www.EricaRidley.com/books

ABOUT THE AUTHOR

Erica Ridley is a *New York Times* and *USA Today* best-selling author of witty, feel-good historical romance novels, including THE DUKE HEIST, featuring the Wild Wynchesters. Why seduce a duke the normal way, when you can accidentally kidnap one in an elaborately planned heist?

In the *12 Dukes of Christmas* series, enjoy witty, heartwarming Regency romps nestled in a picturesque snow-covered village. After all, nothing heats up a winter night quite like finding oneself in the arms of a duke!

Two popular series, the *Dukes of War* and *Rogues to Riches*, feature roguish peers and dashing war heroes who find love amongst the splendor and madness of Regency England.

When not reading or writing romances, Erica can be found eating couscous in Africa, zip-lining through rainforests in Central America, or getting hopelessly lost in the middle of Budapest.

Let's be friends! Find Erica on:
www.EricaRidley.com